INA ZENELI

Looking Death in the Eyes

A Tale of Dreams, Shadows, and Divine Presence

"Don't fight darkness—bring the light, and darkness will disappear."

MAHARISHI MAHESH YOGI

Contents

Preface

Preface: Looking Death in the Eyes

When I first started writing this book, my intention was to share a story based strongly on a true tale of survival amid struggle, a narrative that weaves both the mystical and the diabolic, the angelic and the magical. As the pages of this novel unfold, you'll find a journey that transcends the boundaries of ordinary experiences.

Genre and Audience:

  Title: Looking Death in the Eyes

This inspiring novel is authored by Rachel, a cancer survivor who unveils her remarkable journey of battling the disease while unearthing hope and resilience in the midst of adversity. This is a book that speaks to all ages, for the themes within it resonate universally.

Navigating the Darkness:

  Rachel's story commences with the shattering news of her cancer diagnosis, sending tremors of shock and fear rippling through her world. As the reality of her situation takes hold, she embarks on an emotional journey to reconcile with this new chapter of her life. In the pages that follow, you'll accompany Rachel through the unpredictable terrain of treatment, tracing the lines of her emotions from her first time diagnosed with cancer to the other phases of her ups and downs.

A Glimmer of Light:

The book not only documents the toll cancer exacts on the body and soul but also underscores the vital importance of unwavering support and encouragement. Through the steadfast love of her dear ones and the dedication of her medical team, Rachel's narrative is a poignant reminder that no battle is fought alone.

Embracing Hope Amidst Darkness:

At the heart of it all is Rachel's unyielding spirit and determination. Faced with the specter of cancer, she chooses not to succumb to its shadow but instead to embrace the glimmers of hope and positivity that thread through even the darkest of times.

As you traverse these pages, you'll also encounter a series of extraordinary occurrences—brushes with a shadowy presence, encounters with angels, and dreams that morph into reality. This novel invites you to explore the boundary between the mystical and the mundane, to contemplate the power of belief in both magic and curses.

In writing this book, I've poured my heart and soul into each word, hoping that Rachel's story will illuminate your own path and remind you that, *even in the most challenging moments, hope remains our constant companion.* Her journey embodies the strength of the human spirit and the indomitable force of love and support during times of darkness.

Acknowledgement

In this section, I extend my heartfelt gratitude and appreciation to the individuals and groups who have wholeheartedly supported and contributed to my journey in bringing this book to life:

Family and Friends: My deepest appreciation goes to my family for their unwavering encouragement, profound understanding, and endless patience. Your belief in me has been a constant source of inspiration.

Editors: I am profoundly grateful to the Reedsy editor, Grammarly Go, and ChatGpt, remarkable and free tools, which have played an instrumental role in formatting my book; grammar, and structure. It transformed my manuscript into a beautiful work of art, enhancing its aesthetic appeal and final form. (My story is not a source from Al's content but authentically created by me).

Early Readers and Precious Suggestions: To my early readers, your invaluable insights and suggestions have been a guiding light throughout this process. Your feedback and thoughtful contributions have made this book what it is today.

Special Thanks: A heartfelt thank you to Klaudia Hazizaj, Fiorentina Xhangolli, Xhulia Hazizaj, and Ermira Kastrioti, for their exceptional and unwavering support. Your contributions have transcended a huge help, and your emotional encouragement has been a driving force. My gratitude extends to each of you, and I extend a playful apology for my late-night and early-morning messages.

Inspiration: I draw inspiration from the captivating pages of "THE HOUSEMAID" by Freida McFadden. This extraordinary work has provided invaluable insights into crafting compelling characters, writing evocative descriptions, and creating powerful dialogues.

Personal Reflections: This journey has been punctuated with pauses, as I navigated through the emotional depths experienced by Rachel and her family. The pain and resilience portrayed compelled me to pause, reflect, and continue with renewed determination.

For Future Readers: To the readers who will embark on this journey, I extend my heartfelt gratitude. Your decision to engage with this novel, born from the influence of a special person who prefers to remain private, humbles me.

This book is a testament to the power of collective effort, inspiration, and the incredible impact of unwavering support. To each of you, thank you for being a part of this journey.

Prologue

Throughout my life, I used to think that the moment of dying was something far off in the distant future. But you know what? You can't really predict what lies ahead, can you? Back when we were just kids, my cousin used to playfully wish that I wouldn't make it past 25, casting playful spells and such. Now, I've crossed that milestone and I'm still here, alive and kicking.

Vividly, can recall from my teenage years, two dreams that have stayed with me like permanent imprints. In those dreams, I saw a figure, maybe an angel, maybe God. I couldn't quite put a shape or title to it, but it radiated something divine. It gave me a warning, something foreboding about my future. I didn't catch all the exact words, but it left me with a lingering sense that I should always be prepared for whatever life throws my way.

Now, let's bring things down to reality. Here I am, 27 years old, grappling with an enigma. I'm beginning to feel that my marriage and life have lost their luster like they're fading. I watch my husband come home from work, but it feels like we've lost that connection. All he talks about is his female boss, and even if he says he can't stand her, I can't help but think, "If a man keeps talking about a woman, even if it's negative, maybe there's something more." But I know it's not just about her; I just don't want to admit it.

Things have been changing. We're not laughing or having fun together anymore. I got tired of fighting and arguing, so silence settled between us in our once-bustling apartment. However, I have the greatest gift of all – my son, who brings a smile to my face and gives purpose to my existence.

I couldn't find anything suspicious on his phone, not a trace. It was almost too clean, and that gave me an uneasy feeling. And then, out of nowhere, something unpredictable and uncontrollable entered our lives. It was a really sad event that broke everything. It felt like, life was telling both of us to wake up from our sleep…something really shocking was going to happen…

One

Chapter 1

As the sun began to peek through my window, I slowly opened my eyes, realizing it was time to wake up. It was just another day, or so I thought.

But then I remembered that I had a doctor's appointment scheduled for later that morning. Suddenly, my nerves kicked in, and a knot formed in my stomach. What if the doctor found something wrong? What if I needed surgery or lifelong medication? I was only 27 years old.

I got out of bed and began my usual morning routine, brushing my teeth, washing my face, and getting dressed. With every passing moment, my heart raced faster.

As I stepped outside and made my way to the doctor's office, the knot in my stomach grew tighter. All these thoughts swirled in my head, and I couldn't escape them.

In the reception area, I tried to calm myself down by taking deep breaths, but it didn't seem to be working. The minutes dragged on.

Finally, it was my turn to see the doctor. I walked into the exam room, took a deep breath, and tried to focus on what the doctor was saying. But his words were a jumble, and I couldn't make sense of them.

Leaving the doctor's office, I felt numb. It wasn't until I was alone with my husband in the elevator that the weight of the doctor's words hit me like a ton of bricks. I couldn't believe what I had just heard. All the emotions I had been trying to suppress flooded over me, and I crashed into the elevator's door, sobbing uncontrollably.

I rushed towards the elevator, struggling to breathe in the darkness. My body trembled, and I fell to my knees, feeling a numbing sensation I couldn't comprehend. I thought it was impossible, like a dream or a nightmare. Was I really going through this, or was it all in my head?

When I looked up, my eyes met his, and I asked, "What is it?"

In a state of shock, I couldn't grasp what was happening. Did the doctor just say I had cancer?

My husband looked at me with concern and compassion, but he didn't say anything. He knew that sometimes, in moments like these, words just don't suffice. All I could do was cry and release the shock and sadness that had been building inside me.

After receiving the devastating news about my health, my husband and I sat in silence in the car on the way home. The air was heavy with the weight of the news. Suddenly, a reckless driver nearly collided with our car, causing my husband to slam on the brakes and shout angrily at the driver.

"Can't you see? Don't you know how to drive?" He yelled at the motorcycle driver as if it was his fault for what was happening.

His voice was filled with frustration and fear. At least he could let out a scream; it sometimes helps in those situations.

We pulled into a coffee bar to try and calm ourselves before facing our son, but the silence hung between us.

In a trembling voice, I ordered, "Can I have a cocoa, please?" Meanwhile, my husband ordered water. His face was covered in a shadow of shock and worry. As we sat there, I tried to hide my tears, but they flowed freely despite my efforts. I waited for my husband to comfort me, to tell me everything would be okay. Instead, he lashed out in frustration and anger.

"Stop crying!" he barked at me, his words sharp and cruel.

It was a side of him that I had rarely seen before, and it only added to the chaos and despair that had settled over us. I tried to ask him what would happen next, what we would do, but he could only repeat the question back to me, his voice filled with disbelief.

"What's happening? Why is this happening to us?" he shouted, his words tinged with fear and desperation putting his head down and holding it with both of his hands.

"It was as if the world had turned against us, and we were alone amid the chaos. The whole experience was overwhelming, suffocating, and heartbreaking. Both of us eventually came to realize that the mass present before I became pregnant with my first son was not simply feces, as a mediocre doctor who was unable to read an ultrasound had suggested, but a tumor mass. Miraculously and fortunately, it did not grow during my pregnancy; otherwise, I would have lost my greatest love, my son.

"I didn't lose you; you're still here with us. A miracle that arrived at just the right moment, bringing joy and strengthening our family. 'God has His plans,' I've always believed that, and perhaps this time, He's doing the same."

For a while, something didn't feel quite right in our relationship. Each day passed like any other, without us fully appreciating life's gifts right in front of us.

With all these thoughts racing through my mind, I took a deep breath and made a sincere and faithful promise to myself: "I will never give up. I will fight every last breath left in me… for you… for us…"

* * *

Going back in time, one year ago when we were planning to have a child. We did all the tests to make sure that everything was OK, as I had more than one year not able to. Now, all the previews' events unfolded, and all these occurrences began to connect and make sense. How was it possible that this tumor was growing slowly inside me? How I didn't even realize it until my delivery doctor struggled during the birth procedure? Even though almost ten or eleven months had passed since the birth? Everything was being explained, yet what I didn't understand was, how an assumed ultrasound specialist could just see it as a harmless cyst! How? Can someone explain this bullshit to me?

But inside me it was a feeling that something was not right, something bad was going to happen. I remember those scary nights from the past, haunted by the same creepy dream. It's like a nightmare that won't let go of my thoughts. This dream is a never-ending loop of horror that plays in my mind. Even now, when I try to remember it, a shiver of fear runs down my spine.

It always happened in my aunt's old house in the mysterious town of Gramsh. In the dream, I'd leave her house and step into the cold, dark night. I'd cautiously move down a shadowy hallway, where a strange whisper urged me to keep going. It wasn't just words; it was a ghostly murmur that sent shivers down my spine and made me break into a cold sweat.

As I went further, the air got colder, and the hallway seemed to stretch on forever. Then, in the dim, eerie light, I'd see her: my cousins' long-gone grandmother. She stood at the corner of the hallway, her eyes locked onto mine, her gaze piercing me like a chilling breeze. She looked so real, bathed in an unnatural glow. The old woman wore a black headscarf, which contrasted with her smiling face—a disturbing mix of happiness and something malevolent underneath.

All of a sudden, the feeling around me would change. A strange and eerie voice, not from this world, would echo out. It was as if it came from a place beyond our understanding. "I will take you with me," it would say, and these words had a dark, ominous tone that seemed to fill the entire house, making the walls shake as if they were afraid of something in the darkness.

The scariest part was her hand – it was bony and thin, reaching out desperately to grab me. I fought with all my strength, pushing back against her attempts to claim me. "You can't take me! You can't take me!" I would cry out, these words becoming a desperate chant to keep the looming figure of death at bay.

The struggle went on, a battle of wills in a strange world until I managed to push her away, freeing myself from her grasp. Her smile, which had seemed friendly before, turned into a sinister grin, a brief moment of evil triumph before disappearing into nothingness.

And then, just as suddenly as it had all begun, the dream would fade away, leaving me breathless and drenched in cold sweat. I was left with the mysteries of these horrors that exist beyond what we can see in the real world.

The dream paused, and it felt like ages before I gathered the courage to talk to my mother about it. Those sleepless nights had left me tired and afraid to close my eyes each night. My hands were shaky as I dialed her number, and I explained the nightly terrors that had haunted me for so long.

My mother's voice, a comforting presence, came through the phone after a moment of silence. "You should find a way to bring peace to her troubled soul," she said gently. "Maybe leaving a small offering or some money at her grave could help calm her."

Her words made sense to me. With a newfound determination, I decided to put an end to the restless spirit that plagued my dreams. Little did I know that this journey would lead me to uncover the unsettling truth behind those ghostly figures and the sinister whispers that echoed in the darkness.

* * *

The situation became more urgent, and we realized it was getting late. We knew we had to pick up the baby from the nanny, so Kenneth hurriedly pushed his chair back and went to the waiter. I watched him for a moment, noting his confident and proud walk. Proud of himself, brave, and ready to challenge even armies.

But now, he seemed defeated, walking with his head down. I reached out and held his hand, offering a forced smile.

"We are strong, honey, believe me, we are strong!"

After he paid for the drinks, we headed to Nannie's house," I said firmly, both to myself and silently to my son, even though he couldn't hear my thoughts.

"I long to witness your growth, to be with you in every step. I can't bear the thought of losing you, my dearest one. Mommy will fight for you until the end," I declared to myself.

The moment I arrived at my nanny's house, I greeted her and held my son close, hugging him tightly. In those moments, my eyes filled with tears.

Whispering to my son, I said, "I love you, my life. I can't live without your smile. You are my light. I want to see you grow up and become a happy and healthy man."

I hugged him tightly to hold back my tears, but they were ready to flow. I had to be strong, for Liam's sake; he deserved it. He didn't know what life was or what it brought. Liam knew that his mother loved him and that she was the strongest woman in the world. She was a mother, and mothers moved mountains for their children. That night, we slept side by side, seeking solace in each other's arms.

* * *

The next day, in the morning, after we sent our son to the daycare, we had to meet a specialist recommended by our gynecologist to get a better diagnosis. After that, I needed to have a more detailed MRI to see the size and what exactly it was, in short, a confirmation.

And there we were, at the state hospital, to meet this specialist doctor. And so, we found ourselves at the gates of the state hospital. The state hospital in Tirane loomed before us like a scene from the Gothic tale, an ominous sight with an unending queue both outside and inside, filled with anxious souls clutching their bags as if they were bracing themselves for an unknown trial. Staring at the situation with crowded people pushing each other and screaming at the police at the hospital doors, made me feel hopeless and lost. As we finally gained entry, the atmosphere felt like a purgatory, resembling a haunting tableau that could send shivers down one's spine...

Summoning our courage, my husband Kenneth spoke to the doctor:

"Hello, doctor! We're here because a friend of yours recommended us to see you for a more detailed examination," Kenneth said.

"Yes," the doctor confirmed and made space for us to enter.

The doctor, a tall man in his fifties, shared his life story about how he had graduated in England and had grown tired of working in Albania without feeling appreciated. He expressed a desire to return there and find a job, still feeling a sense of responsibility for his country and people. It was as if he were confessing his guilt at leaving, though there was little else he could do.

Then, he inquired about the location of the mass and requested, "You need to step outside so, I can examine your wife."

I stood there, frozen and uncomfortable, wondering what would happen next. How would he check on me, when there was only one bed and one chair in the room?!

"What was just happening?" I thought, my confusion giving way to courage.

With determination building up inside me, I thought of the resilience of strong women who had faced much more than this. The doctor's gentle yet unwavering voice broke through my thoughts.

"Please, lie down," he instructed in a soft voice. "We need to check if the mass is soft or hard," he stated firmly.

As I lay down, I couldn't help but wonder how he would approach this. A deep discomfort settled in those moments, and I felt anxious.

"Take off your pants because I need to check in the rectum to take the measurement. Please stay calm; we will finish very soon," he reassured, attempting to calm me down.

An indescribable discomfort gripped me tightly, and anxiety knotted in my stomach. He explained the necessity of checking the rectum to understand the nature of the mass, putting in effort to soothe my doubts in those moments.

And so, we embarked on the procedure, which proved to be both painful and uncomfortable. As seconds stretched, time seemed to play a cruel joke, stretching each second into an eternity. I took deep breaths and repeated to myself over and over again:

"You've got this!"
   "You're almost there!"
   "It will be over soon!"

In a calm and quiet voice, he said, "Now, please stand up and get dressed."

I felt a sense of relief and quickly put on my pants, almost like I was in a hurry. Then it was time to call my husband into the room. As Kenneth walked up to the doctor, he said:

"As I suspected, the mass is hard, but we'll need an MRI for a closer look," he said confidently.

"Thank you for your time, doctor," Kenneth replied.

"Of course, we gave some money to the doctor, as it's the custom in Albania. I wasn't sure why we went to him when we needed an MRI anyway. Maybe it was just about giving money? These were the thoughts my husband and I shared as we walked, getting ready for the day ahead. The MRI was scheduled for the next day. It was also time for work – but could I even manage to go to work?"

* * *

I stood there, right at the entrance of my workplace – a big, tall building. I felt incredibly small, like an ant in a huge world. Before I even took a step inside, I took a really deep breath.

I worked in the human resources department of a customer service call center company. I was on the hiring team. When I got there, I went to the manager and asked if we could talk when she had some time. As I walked through the halls, I remembered the lively atmosphere. Even though it could be tiring, that job made me feel like I was part of something important. I felt valued, like a piece of a big puzzle with more than 500 employees. But even with all this support, it was really hard to talk about what I was going through. It felt incredibly hard. Still, I held onto a little hope, at least until the detailed MRI.

I went up to the second floor, where I recognized some faces. And there she was, coming toward me – Jonna. Her eyes showed concern and a glimmer of understanding that something was wrong. With a heavy heart, I looked down, a clear sign of how sad I felt.

As Jonna approached, her concerned expression urged me to gather my courage and share the difficult news. I spoke in hushed tones as if revealing a secret, saying, "Jonna, we need to talk."

We located a quiet corner on the second floor and started our conversation. Jonna wasn't just my boss; she was also someone I could trust and confide in. She had a unique blend of strength and kindness. With long, black hair, a tall and slim figure, and a friendly face, she exemplified leadership and compassion. Her eyes, dark and understanding, seemed to perceive things beyond words. Jonna embodied both authority and a warm heart.

"Rachel, how did your doctor's visit go?" Her voice carried concern as if she could sense that something was troubling me.

"It didn't go well, Jonna," I replied, my tone reflecting sadness as I looked downward.

"Why? What happened?" She inquired, her worried eyes never leaving me.

"I have a tumor," I admitted, my voice trembling. "I still need to have an MRI to get more details," I whispered, revealing the painful truth.
I confessed, my words heavy with a hidden truth I hadn't shared with anyone before. It felt like the walls around me were protectors, keeping my vulnerable secret from the world.

She looked shocked, like a sudden loud noise. But her kind response gave me a bit of hope in this uncertain world.

To her surprise, she asked, "What are you saying? Did you talk to a doctor? Maybe it's not something to worry about. Check it out once, don't stress without knowing for sure. Whatever it is, you're young, only 27 years old. You're strong and brave. Your spirit is like a fortress that can withstand the toughest storms!"

"Thank you, Jonna. I appreciate your support," I smiled on the outside, pretending that everything was okay. But inside, I felt lost and afraid. I was scared to death because death felt like it was coming for me, and I wasn't prepared for it. Well, no one ever is. My emotions were like a raging fire, leaving me in the dark, filled with doubts and worries. My hands were shaking and sweating at the same time.

The girls in the office, all three of them, knew I had a gynecologist appointment. As soon as I opened the office door, their eyes were on me. They were looking for answers that I couldn't keep from them for much longer.

Greta, always eager, spoke up first: "Rachel, how did the doctor's visit go? What did they say?"

Seeing their worried expressions, I knew I couldn't keep it a secret. I sat down, took a deep breath, and with tears in my eyes, I said, "I have a tumor. I don't know more details, but we'll find out tomorrow with an MRI."

Greta, Sido, and Kim rushed and hugged me with their love, like a shield from the storm of uncertainty that had just begun. I stayed in my chair, and the tears kept flowing. I couldn't stop them; it was like a faucet that I couldn't turn off. I was caught in an emotional storm.

While I couldn't stop crying, a coordinator who needed to see us came into the room. When she saw the situation, she said "sorry" quietly and stepped back, like a respectful intruder. She closed the door with a soft click, giving us a moment of privacy.

* * *

The following day, I found myself in a private German hospital, all set for an MRI scan. This private hospital was different from the public one – everything was normal, but it cost over $300 for each scan, which was quite expensive compared to Albania.

When the nurse tried to place a tube in my arm, it became clear that she didn't know how to do it. She poked me multiple times, making me bleed. But then, a young and good-looking MRI specialist stepped in and told the nurse, "Let me do it." He managed to get the tube in on the first try and told me that the scan would begin in ten minutes.

Yes, that big MRI machine on the inside has a small, tight space. I didn't like it, and I don't think anyone does. I'm also scared of needles, but here I am with a tube in my arm.

As I entered the large, cold room, fear crept over me, sending shivers down my spine. It was like a chilling and frightening gust of wind. However, the doctor reassured me that I could talk to him through the headphones if I felt scared during the scan. He also mentioned that there would be music playing to help me relax.

I've always been scared of small, enclosed spaces, which can sometimes trigger panic. But as I entered the narrow tunnel with flashing lights, the doctor's voice in my headphones calmed me down. I had to lie completely still for what felt like an eternity, like a statue frozen in time. The scan needed about thirty minutes to capture all the details of my organs, and the tube was there for that purpose.

At last, the scan was over.

Kenneth would get the MRI results the next day, but their expressions didn't look good. My work in Human Resources had taught me a lot about reading people's body language, and their gestures told me it wasn't good news, or at least that's what I thought.

At that moment, it felt like my heart had stopped. We had just confirmed that there was a tumor in my body. The weight of the whole world seemed to press down on Kenneth's shoulders. The news of a tumor hit me hard, and I was left trembling and speechless, not sure how to react.

Back at home, I looked at my 11-month-old son. I had to take a deep breath, trying to hold back the tears that wanted to burst out. The pain in my heart was unbearable like someone was scraping their nails across it. But I knew I had to stay strong for my family. The wait for the doctor's response would be agonizing, but I had to hold on to hope and believe that everything would be okay.

After dinner, we went to bed, both of us needing…

I was fast asleep in my room, or so I thought. Suddenly, I was overwhelmed by an unexplainable sense of fear. It was like someone, or something, was watching me. I tried to shake off the feeling and go back to sleep, but it was impossible. The presence felt stronger and more sinister with each passing moment. I was cold and filled with anxiety.

I woke up, and to my terror, I saw a dark, shadowy figure near the bedroom door. It had no clear shape, but I could sense its evil energy. I was so scared that I couldn't move or scream for help.

The shadow appeared to be waiting for something, and it wanted me. I felt its intense, everlasting anger. I wanted to scream, run away, and do anything to escape, but my body wouldn't obey.

Tears streamed down my face, and I could barely say my husband's name, "Kenneth, please hold me, I need you, please."

He rushed to my side and held me tightly as I trembled with fear. "It's okay," he whispered, hugging me even tighter. "I'm here."

I held onto him tightly, thankful for his comforting presence and the security it provided in those moments. I eventually drifted into slumber, a sense of protection enveloping me. However, the memory of the ominous figure lingered, leaving me anxious because I was certain it would come back…

Two

Chapter 2

Yesterday afternoon, the doctor didn't provide an answer after a nerve-wracking wait. With uncertainty looming, I decided to stick to my routine, heading to my workplace, a dynamic building spanning multiple floors.

The first floor featured a spacious hall with operators, an office, restrooms, and an indoor bar where we gathered for drinks and lunch. Moving up to the second floor, you'd find a smaller hall with more operators, as well as additional offices. This floor housed the human resources department and the company administrator, along with two training rooms. The third floor, too, accommodated operators and offices.

Working in this company was a unique experience. The office itself was inviting, with ample natural light pouring in through large windows and a well-thought-out layout that made it easy to navigate. Yet, it wasn't just the physical space that set it apart. The people who worked there formed a tight-knit team that supported each other through thick and thin. They were more than colleagues; they were a close-knit family. They excelled in communication, knowing when to lend an ear and when to respect personal space. This office was a prime example of teamwork, effective management, and continuous growth. While it was formerly known as IDS Inbound, it has since become a part of Comdata, a customer management BPO provider headquartered in Corsica, Italy. One thing was certain, the people and the atmosphere of that office would forever hold a special place in my heart.

Despite feeling emotionally drained, I forced myself to smile when I arrived at the bar.

"Hi," I greeted warmly, as was my habit. "Could I please have a coffee, and also a juice with beets, carrots, and apples?"

The bartender seemed taken aback by my order. "Oh, embracing a healthier diet, are we?" she inquired.

"Yes, exactly," I affirmed with a smile, concealing my inner pain.

That day was like any other day at our office. There were four recruiters - three for inbound services and one for outbound. I had many interviews with various candidates because we always had to make a class with fifteen newcomers almost every two weeks. Everything was going well, and we were professionals who always welcomed our candidates. Greta was using the interview chair that had mechanics to move it up and down, but I was never good with it.

"Rachel, could you get the next interview, please?" Greta asked politely.

"Sure, I can," I smiled back.

We had to take the candidates from the first floor to the second floor where our office was located. While being polite and professional, I tried to sit on the chair, but it was so high that I almost fell. I smiled and grabbed the chair, practically jumping into it. I can laugh at myself now when I remember that.

I posed the candidate with routine questions during the interview, yet his responses were peculiar. For instance, when I inquired about his graduation status, his answer took a serious turn.

"I hold a master's degree, much like a Prime Minister," he stated with sincerity.

The university he mentioned, however, was exclusively dedicated to engineering and bore no relevance to the political field.

In our country, there was no such department or specialization. How, then, could one claim a Prime Minister's background? The notion was both amusing and incredibly absurd.

I lowered my head and inquired, "Are you absolutely certain this aligns with your academic field?"

"Absolutely," he affirmed with a persuasive undertone.

"Hmm! That's both amusing and incredibly silly," I remarked, lowering my head, and questioned, "Are you certain this falls within your field of study?"

"Indeed," he replied convincingly.

She couldn't be any more serious and couldn't control her laughter. At that moment, Greta nudged her desk forward and mumbled, "Apologies," her hand shielding her face.

Swinging the door open, she exited, allowing me to resume the interview. I outlined various steps, explaining that I would notify him of the outcome within two weeks if selected. Otherwise, he would not be contacted.

Later, I heard that something had happened to Greta. I walked to the reception area, seeking answers from one of the girls.

I smiled and asked, "Could you describe how Greta fell down the stairs?"

With my eyes half-closed, as if beginning an investigation, I inquired, "And how did she react after the fall?"

She chuckled and replied, "She was laughing so hard that she didn't notice the stairs, and she stumbled. After standing up, she said, 'Rachel, how can you be so serious?' She had tears in her eyes, all while still laughing."

* * *

Thus, another workday concluded. Upon arriving home in the afternoon, I found my husband seated in a corner. His expression was etched with distress and darkness. I cannot even find the right words to describe it, that face was bearing the weight of hardship and a lot of emotions simultaneously.

"The MRI results came in, and they confirmed it was a tumor. Now we need to figure out what to do. The specialist also confirmed that the mass was deeply hidden, making surgery in Albania too risky."

At that moment, Albania didn't seem like the right place of hope.

He made his decision clear without giving me a chance to answer, stating, "Today, the tickets in Italy will be arranged."

I sat down on the couch, shocked.

"But how long will we stay there?" I asked, concerned about our small, fragile, and happy son.

"Oh, that smile filled me with life at every moment. How could I stay without him, without seeing him, without embracing him, without taking care of him?"

"What about our son?" I said, trying to reassure him.

"Your Mom will take care of him," he replied, his tone irritated. "Do you think she can? But in these circumstances, there's nothing else she can do."

"What are you talking about? Don't make baseless accusations, please, enough," I responded, annoyed.

"I need to discuss this at work and sort everything out," I whispered to myself. I only had one week to get everything ready.

* * *

The next day, my manager was really understanding. She said, "Just go to Italy and focus on your health; we'll handle everything else." Her words were like a gentle hug during a very dark time.

That week, the one right after I got that awful news, remains vivid in my memory. It felt like a heavy darkness had covered the world, making it hard to see anything.

In that scary moment, I had an urge to reach out to someone I thought I had left behind a decade ago. This person had a special way of making me smile, even during the toughest times. But in the end, I never truly understood what happened between us. I never grasped his feelings or why he was with me for a while and then everything changed. I was someone who never allowed others to hurt me, so I distanced myself from him. Well, however, it's a story that deserves its own telling...

Now, I needed him: his comforting presence, his humor, or simply his eyes that spoke volumes without words.

So, I made a bold decision, something I had never dared to do before. I needed answers: how, why, or what had happened between us? The burden of not knowing and the ache of longing had become too much to bear.

I thought about sending a message on Facebook without revealing my identity, referring to myself in the third person. The burning questions that had haunted me for years were, 'Did he ever have any feelings for me?' How would he react if he knew I had limited time left? Did he still remember me, or had I faded from his thoughts?

From 2008 to 2017, there had been no significant contact—no signs, no news, nothing at all. And there I sat, taking a risk, my fingers trembling as I typed. With a deep breath, I started to write.

"Hello, I am someone from your past. I want to share something about your ex-girlfriend from 2008 when you were both in high school. I feel it's important to let you know that she is seriously ill and is scheduled to undergo surgery in Italy. It's possible you might not cross paths again, even though much time has passed since you last saw each other. She would greatly appreciate it if you could address these questions for her":

"Did you ever think about her over all these years? Did you genuinely love her, or was it just a game to you?"

On his end, there was silence—just silence. Meanwhile, he read all the messages but didn't reply. The ache was almost unbearable. At that moment, I felt as if I could burst into tears as if there was nothing left.

Summoning courage, I continued, "Do you recall the song you dedicated to me when we broke up? Do you still stand by the words, wishing for my eternal happiness? What would it cost you to share just that much? What significance did I hold in your life? Can you grasp that my time on this earth might be nearing its close? Please, I only seek that from you—nothing else. Please, answer me."

After a series of probing questions followed by a profound silence, a distant typing motion heralded the birth of a message.

"Would he admit that he still thinks about me? Would my illness make him worried? Would he care if I disappeared or got really sick?" I kept thinking about these things.

Then, I got a response with just question marks and exclamation points: "?????!!!!!!"

Tears cascaded down my cheeks, transforming the office into a Topsy-turvy world where chairs clung to the ceiling and windows had vanished. I felt suffocated, crushed beneath the burden of unrequited emotions. My head fell into my hand as I drew a trembling breath. He never loved me, not then, not ever. The pain was profound, an ever-bleeding wound. I couldn't hate him; it wasn't in my nature. He was a chapter of the past, destined to linger in the bittersweet memories of what might have been.

It was a sunny beautiful day so, Greta and I decided to have lunch by the lake to escape from our worries. We needed each other's company to feel better. We sat on the dry grass, watching ducks peacefully swim on the lake. Then, Greta had an idea. She smiled and asked, "Rachel, want to have a smoke with me?"

Inhaling deeply, I responded, "Oh, certainly. In moments like these, I'd smoke something stronger than this." Our laughter was a brief escape from the enveloping sorrow.

Two shattered souls sought refuge in each other's presence. Greta had parted ways with her fiancé, a relationship that had spanned many years, but it had its complications, perhaps health-related. Life, as we both knew, had its unpredictable ways—it could embrace you and then, without warning, toss you into an abyss.

"Ray, I did some Facebook snooping about your ex," Greta started gently, trying not to hurt me more.

"What did you find?" I asked, feeling anxious.

"He's engaged, and that's probably why he didn't respond," Greta explained. I looked down and stared at the lake.

"So many years have passed. It's normal for him to move on. I'm truly happy for him," I said with a sigh. My heart felt heavy, a mix of sadness and understanding.

Greta, always like reading my spirit, said, "I know, Rachel. First love never really fades, no matter how much time goes by, and it hurts just the same."

Sitting by the lake, I finally let my held-back tears flow. I cried not just for the love I lost but also for all the dreams that would remain unfulfilled.

In that moment of vulnerability, Greta held me close, offering the comfort I needed. Our tears mixed with the setting sun's reflection on the water as if nature itself shared in our sadness.

Together, we found strength in each other's presence. We weren't alone, and our journey to heal had just started, promising both tears and laughter along the way.

After lunch, we went back to work. The days before my trip to Italy were getting closer, and it made me more and more anxious. I felt like something was squeezing my stomach so hard that I could barely breathe.

I tried hard to stay calm, but then I saw my son, Liam, playing in the kitchen. He meant everything to me. The idea of leaving him with no clear plan to return was really painful. How could I handle being away from him? I didn't know.

When it was time to leave my parents' house, I held onto my son, not wanting to say goodbye. My voice shook as I whispered, "I love you." It was so hard, but I had to let go…

Three

Chapter 3

In the morning, we drove to the airport in our car, and my brother-in-law would take charge of parking it in Gramsh. Kenneth strove to appear strong, concealing the worry and uncertainty that he grappled with internally. He endeavored to consider every possible option, both for me and for us. With an attempt at a smile, he suggested,

"Let's grab a coffee until it's time for us to check in."

We settled at a small table in the 'Mother Teresa' Airport in Tirane. Typically, the prices there ran high, but our hands were tied. The espresso had become an indispensable part of our morning ritual; it was the jolt we needed to awaken. Gazing into his eyes with their long, dark lashes, I discerned the weight of the burden he bore. But he wasn't alone, and neither was I. We had each other. I yearned to convey the gravity of this connection. Observing his hand resting on the table—slender, with those long, enticing fingers that had always beckoned me to caress them—I extended my own hand, placing it gently atop his.

"We are strong, with God's help, everything will be fine," I whispered softly.

Startled and somewhat irked, he turned his head to the left and retorted, "God? Which God are you referring to? If He truly existed, none of this would have occurred. Spare me talk of God! He's a nonexistent entity. I'm an atheist; I don't believe in God."

In that moment, resolute and steady, I replied in a normal voice, "I believe, and I'll never cease to believe!"

Recognizing that his words stemmed from frustration and fear, I added with a faint smile, "Let's proceed step by step and entrust our worries into His hands."

Finally, it was time to board the plane. We finished the check-in process and waited for our plane to leave. Our plane came closer. Our seats were by the wings. Even though it wasn't my first flight, I'd still be scared even if it was my thousandth. I'm just a fearful person. When I sat in my seat, I held onto the armrests tightly and closed my eyes, not wanting to see the plane take off. Kenneth sensed that I was scared and held my hand firmly, smiling to reassure me. He said, "Don't be afraid. When you're scared, just hold my hand."

Then, the moment came when the plane started to land. I was already scared of takeoff and flying. But the pilot was very skilled and landed the plane smoothly. I knew that Kenneth's cousin Leo was waiting for us on the other side of the airport. Even though we were a bit tired, the Italians were quick to check our documents, so we didn't have to wait for a long time.

I've always admired their culture. They are warm and kind, and they have a contagious energy that makes you laugh easily. As I rushed from the airport, I greeted Leo. I hid behind the familiar mask that hardly ever leaves me, especially when I'm around other people — "the smile." This smile was like my shield, protecting me from every word and hiding the painful truths behind it. It's important never to let them see your sadness, your hard struggle, or the deep fear hidden behind tall walls.

"How have you been, Leo?" I asked with a smile that tried to look natural. "Thank you for being here," I added.

"Hey, cousin," Kenneth said.

"I'm good. How about you?" Leo asked, even though he knew what was happening.

My eyes dropped for a moment, but I quickly raised my head, hiding everything behind a practiced smile. We got into the car and drove to their house. I was really looking forward to some food; I was hungry and tired.

Kenneth and Leo sat in the front seats, and I found myself alone in the back. As I looked out of the window, I saw a long stretch of highway. Time passed, and their voices became a distant sound. I rested my head against the window and let my mind wander, thinking about my son. These thoughts filled my mind, like heavy rain. "Can we find a good surgeon here? How much will it cost? And if we can't find one? What will happen to me?"

I lost track of time, the exchange of their voices becoming inaudible background noise. Sunlight intensified the blonde strands of hair, and the green hue of my eyes seemed to amplify under its touch. Yet, the rays felt like they were warming more than just my physical form—my heart, my thoughts, even my soul that had become marooned in a cold, solitary place.

Abruptly, a hand jolted my body, and his voice whispered, "Rachel, we've arrived."

I clutched my chest, the tendrils of pain washing over my fragile body once more. The ceaseless skirmish against cancer had drained me of strength, leaving me yearning and desperate for a cure. Yet, a resolute determination surged within; Italy loomed on the horizon, a beacon of hope, a potential remedy that had eluded us thus far, and we pinned our aspirations on it.

We arrived at the address that was written on a worn-out piece of paper. We stood in front of Leo's simple house, with our hopes hanging by a thin thread. To our surprise, the door swung open, and we saw an organized mess inside. A young woman, Nia, was there, and her face showed deep lines of sadness. Her tired eyes looked like they had been through battles, and it felt like we shared a connection of suffering.

"Are you Leo's wife?" I asked softly, my voice filled with understanding.

Nia nodded, her voice barely a whisper. "Yes, I am. Please, come in."

Nia was a woman a few years older than me, but she seemed much older at that moment. She had dark circles under her eyes, and her long, black hair looked messy like she hadn't taken care of it in a while. She was still in her pajamas, even though it was after lunch, and her gaze seemed far away, lost in thought. As I looked at her, I felt deep sympathy for the burden she was carrying.

Stepping inside, the once inviting living room now resembled a battleground of despair. Toys were strewn across the floor, unwashed dishes formed precarious towers in the sink, and an air of neglect lingered heavily. The silence was broken only by the distant cries of a baby from another room.

Leo, Nia's husband, emerged from the kitchen, his face etched with exhaustion—a reflection of the burdens he carried. He had become the caretaker, skillfully juggling the weight of his wife's deteriorating mental health alongside the responsibilities of their infant daughter.

"I apologize for the mess," Leo stated, his voice tinged with weariness. "Nia has been grappling with depression for months now. She can hardly care for herself, let alone our daughter."

My heart sank as I witnessed the weight of Leo's burden. It put my own struggles into perspective, and I exchanged a worried glance with Kenneth. We understood that we could not continue staying for too long in this house, after witnessing all that struggle that was consuming them.

"I... I'll cook something for everyone," Leo offered, his voice laden with weariness. "Please, make yourselves at home."

Gratitude was not enough to say that we felt from them. The heavy silence lingered, suffocating our thoughts as we contemplated the overwhelming darkness that shrouded this household.

As Leo prepared the spaghetti, we began talking about my search for the right surgeon. I shared my hopes and fears, finding tranquility only in a sparkle of hope. Leo listened intently, his eyes reflecting both compassion and the weight of his own struggles.

The aroma of Leo's homemade meal wafted through the room, offering a momentary respite from the gripping tension. We gathered around the table, plates brimming with warmth, our hearts laden with unspoken emotions.

At one poignant instant, Nia's gaze locked with mine. In that fleeting connection, a spark of hope ignited within the depths of her despair. Shadows began to recede, and it was as if I could feel her anguish rather than just witnessing it.

I turned to Kenneth, my voice radiating unshakable determination. "We can't remain passive bystanders, nor can we abandon them. We have to find a solution, Kenneth!" I believed that our paths had intersected for a reason—a chance to extend a hand while navigating our own tempestuous seas.

"Leo needs to understand that he has to help Nia find the right support. She's reaching out for help, can't you see that?" I begged Kenneth.

Suddenly, a loud crash broke the fragile peace in the room. Kenneth and I quickly stood up, looking towards the noise.

In one corner of the room, a broken picture frame was on the floor, its shattered glass reflecting Nia's fragile state. Tears were running down her face as she held onto her daughter, a mix of desperation and fear in her embrace.

I didn't hesitate and went to Nia, speaking to her in a soothing voice filled with understanding. "It's okay, Nia. I'm here for you. You're not alone in this struggle."

Nia's eyes met mine, and at that moment, a glimmer of hope emerged from her despair. The darkness slowly faded, giving way to a glimmer of possibility.

I turned to Kenneth once more, speaking firmly. "We have to find a way to help them, Kenneth. It's our duty."

Kenneth agreed, his determination matching my own. Our own struggles had led us to this point—a chance to bring comfort while fighting our own battles.

"She's reaching out for help, just like I am. Can't you see that?" I added urgency in my voice.

* * *

Days turned into weeks, and I put my heart into doing the house chores, like laundry, cooking, and cleaning. I also took care of her daughter and listened to Nia's problems. But as time went by, I started to feel drained, like I was getting pulled into a whirlpool of overthinking and stress.

Balancing my own struggles with helping Nia and Leo became more and more complicated. It was like the fragile thread holding me together was starting to unravel. I was torn between my commitment to support them and the need to take care of my own mental health.

One morning, things got really intense when Leo and Nia had an argument. Nia got so angry that she almost hit Kenneth and threw the TV remote at Leo. After a long silence, she broke down in tears.

She cried out, "Can't you see, you fool? I'm not well, just like her. I need help. Look at Kenneth - he came all the way from Albania to help her. You should do the same for me. Help me get better. I want to be well. Can't you understand that?"

A heavy silence filled the small apartment, making it difficult to breathe. In those moments, we realized that they needed space to work through their own problems and struggles.

Since then, we went upstairs to Leo's sister's place in the same building. We gathered in her children's room, where they had a cozy sailor-themed bed. We ate spaghetti and drank wine to find comfort. Even though it seemed peaceful, at night, I often couldn't stop crying. I missed my son so much that I had many panic attacks, but I tried to hide them from Kenneth. He couldn't fully understand how a mother feels about her child.

He would often scold me, saying, "Stop acting like a child and grow up!"

I understand it might seem harsh, but that's his way of responding in challenging times. Even though there were moments when I needed someone to lean on for comfort, it wasn't with him. Well, it felt like I couldn't find that with anyone I knew.

I had an appointment with a doctor tomorrow to discuss my cancer. I felt really anxious as I headed to the hospital in the Lombardia Region. My scans and MRI showed the details of my condition, and I was bracing myself for the news I would hear.

When I got to the hospital, they directed me to the office where the medical team in charge of my case was waiting. As I walked into the room, I felt a rush of nervousness mixed with uncertainty. The doctors, a general surgeon, and a neurosurgeon, welcomed me with a mix of concern and determination.

"Well, well, look who's here," the general surgeon exclaimed, his voice infused with a hint of surprise. "You've certainly presented us with quite the challenge."

Sitting uncomfortably, I felt the weight of their words pressing on me. "What options do I have? Can the surgery be performed? Is there any hope?"

The neurosurgeon, well-known for his skill in complex surgeries, leaned in and spoke carefully. "Let's be clear. The tumor's placement between the spine and the hip is a big challenge. We'll have to do everything we can to deal with it."

I felt a mix of fear and determination. I needed to fully understand how serious the situation was and what the risks were.

"Are you saying the surgery can't be done?"

The general surgeon leaned back and looked serious. "Not impossible, but it won't be easy. We'll need both a general surgeon and a neurosurgeon to face this challenge."

Taking a deep breath, I felt the weight of what lay ahead. The seriousness of the situation became clear, but I was determined to fight through it. I asked, "I understand the challenges. What's the next step?"

The neurosurgeon leaned closer, looking directly at me. He said, "First, we need to make a detailed surgical plan. It's a tricky task that requires careful precision."

Many thoughts and feelings rushed through my mind, but I had a strong determination. I said, "I'm ready for whatever it takes. I won't let this tumor beat me."

Sitting in the car, I turned to Kenneth, my voice filled with worry. "We don't have enough money to pay for all these expenses. How can we manage this? It feels like a big challenge."

Kenneth's face showed that he felt the same concerns, but he held my hand with reassurance. "Don't worry, Rachel. We'll figure it out. We won't let money problems stop you from getting the treatment you need. We'll look for help from every possible source and keep fighting to get the support we need."

I nodded, feeling better knowing he was so determined. We couldn't allow money issues to put my recovery in danger, or at least that's what we hoped for.

After we talked, we went for a relaxed walk in Milano, and eventually, we got to Piazza del Duomo. While strolling around the busy square, I couldn't resist trying to take a photo with a friendly pigeon. I was excited and bought some corn from a nearby seller. I held out my hand, thinking it would make a great picture. But when the pigeon's feathers touched my hand unexpectedly, I got scared and let out a loud scream. Everyone in the crowd looked at me with curiosity, making me feel really embarrassed. I quickly pulled my hand back, and I exchanged embarrassed looks with Kenneth and Leo. As if this wasn't enough, a man appeared, holding out his hand, asking for money for the corn. I felt trapped, realizing that what I thought was a simple act of feeding the pigeon came with an unexpected cost. I learned a lesson that day: there's no such thing as a free meal, or in this case, a free picture with a pigeon. The whole incident left me feeling flustered and nervous. We were all tired from the day's events, so we decided it was best to go home and find some comfort and rest after such an exhausting day.

We held on to our last bit of hope, knowing we had one more chance to ease our growing pile of hospital bills. If luck was with us, maybe we could find a way to get help from the government to cover our financial problems. Going through the emergency route at the hospital seemed like a reasonable idea. Many people had tried this before, but we weren't sure if it would work for us now. We came up with a plan for me to pretend I had terrible stomach pain and ask the medical staff for help. We had someone we knew inside the hospital who might be able to guide us.

Feeling anxious, we walked into the emergency room, and I put on a convincing act of being in agony. We waited for what felt like forever, and the blank hospital walls closed in on us. Finally, a nurse called my name, and we went over to her with uncertainty in our faces.

"What seems to be the problem?" the nurse asked, her voice tinged with a mix of curiosity and empathy.

I mustered up all the pain I could in my voice, trying to make it sound genuine. "I'm experiencing severe abdominal pain. It's unbearable. I need help."

She nodded sympathetically, leading us toward the examination area. As the doctor approached, I continued to play my part, my heart pounding with a blend of anxiety and hope.

"Tell me about your symptoms," the doctor inquired, his tone clinical yet attentive.

I grimaced, clutching my abdomen. "It's a sharp, stabbing pain that comes in waves. It's been persistent for days now, and I'm getting worried."

The doctor's brow furrowed as he examined me. "I understand your concern. Let's run some tests and see what we can find."

As we anxiously awaited the results, the minutes ticked by like hours. My mind was a whirlwind of emotions, alternating between anticipation and fear. Would this desperate attempt at seeking support yield any results?

Finally, the doctor returned, holding a clipboard with a serious expression on his face. "The test results are in, and they show some abnormalities. We need to discuss this further."

My heart skipped a beat, and I exchanged a nervous glance with Kenneth. It seemed like our efforts might be paying off.

Sitting in the doctor's office, we listened attentively as he explained the situation. "Your test results indicate a complex tumor, situated between the spine and the hip region. It's a challenging case that requires specialized expertise."

I swallowed hard, my mind racing with the gravity of his words. "What are our options? Can this be treated?"

The doctor sighed, a mix of concern and compassion in his eyes. "Given the complexity, we would need the skills of both a general surgeon and a neurosurgeon to tackle this. It won't be an easy road, but it's not impossible."

My heart sank, the weight of the situation threatening to overwhelm me. "But how can we afford such a complex procedure? The financial burden is already too much."

The doctor leaned forward; his voice filled with empathy. "I understand your concerns. We'll explore every possible avenue to help you access the necessary care. But I won't sugarcoat it – it will require significant resources."

The doctor nodded, a glimmer of hope in his eyes. "I hear your determination. Let's collaborate and explore all available options. We won't rest until we've exhausted every avenue to provide you with the support you need."

I spoke up to clarify, "Do we have any support available from the Italian government, or is that not possible?"

The doctor lowered his head and replied, "Unfortunately, you are not covered by the Italian state's insurance. You will have to cover the expenses out of your pocket."

"I see. And if I may ask, do you have an average of the usual cost for these surgeries?" "Well, it's at least $25,000," he answered with conviction.

"I understand," I replied, swallowing the weight of the information. We expressed our gratitude for their time and support before leaving.

With renewed determination, we left the hospital, the weight of uncertainty still heavy on our shoulders. It was clear that our desperate attempt through the emergency route hadn't yielded the immediate financial assistance we had hoped for. However, the doctors' acknowledgment of the miracle of my healthy pregnancy that now I have a son of 1-year-old despite the tumor. Which now served as a reminder of the resilience and hope that guided us.

A week later, we made a bold decision. Fueled by a relentless pursuit of answers and solutions, we embarked on a plane back to Albania. It was a leap of faith, but we believed that within its borders lay the possibility of a breakthrough. With hearts heavy yet hopeful, we set out on this new chapter, ready to face the challenges that lay ahead and find the solution we so desperately sought.

Four

Chapter 4

When I got back from the airport in Tirane, all I could think about was seeing my son. I missed him so much, and the longing to be with him was overwhelming. We didn't waste any time and went straight home because my parents had brought him there, at least for now. My husband, Kenneth, and I made a decision together to think about having the surgery in Albania, and we held onto a tiny bit of hope. We knew that with the help of my miracle-working aunt and her husband, we might find a way.

They've always been a great help in our lives, and when I say "our lives," I mean everyone in our family. They've consistently been there for us during tough times, providing unwavering support through generations. But my connection with them was special. We shared a bond that's hard to put into words.

I've always looked up to my aunt. She's a role model for me, a shining example of purity, hard work, and intelligence. I wish I could confide in her, tell her, "Aunt Maria, I've tried to be the best version of you, but sometimes, I've fallen short. I'm really sorry."

Standing next to her is her husband, Mark, who has a heart full of kindness. He's always ready to help us in any way he can. Their life has had its share of challenges, but they're always there for each other. I knew that if I ever needed help, they would do everything they could to support me.

My aunt is someone I'm really proud of. She has so many roles – she's a lawyer, a manager, and even a politician. But more than anything, she's strong and caring. Her husband is wise and a writer, which makes them an amazing team. They're like strong pillars of support, not just for me but for everyone who knows them. All I had to do was ask.

I felt really embarrassed when I called my aunt to explain what was going on. I was worried about how she would react and what advice she might give. I didn't want to bother her with my problems. But things had gotten so serious that it was a matter of life and death. So, I had to pick up the phone and call her.

"Hi, Aunt! How are you?" I whispered hesitantly, my fear palpable in my voice.

"Hi, Rachel! I've missed my sweetheart. How are you doing?" she replied warmly, sensing my unease.

Pausing for a moment, I hesitated to share the news, fearing it would cause her pain. "Um… the thing is, I've been diagnosed with… um… a tumor. Despite our attempts in Italy, nothing has yielded results. You're my last hope now." Tears welled in my eyes, struggling to stay confined within my lids.

On the other end of the line, I sensed a mixture of anger, worry, and panic in her voice. "And you're just telling me now?! Seriously? I'm going to find a solution. Do you even realize how precious you are to me?"

She cut off the call, leaving me alone with my thoughts for about half an hour. Then the phone rang again.

"Rachel, I love you. You hold a special place in my heart. We'll do everything in our power to help you. But next time, if there ever is a next time, don't hesitate to call me."

"I'm sorry," I whispered through tears, overwhelmed by guilt. "I just didn't want to burden you with worries. I love you, and I'm so sorry for causing you sadness." With tears streaming down my face, I ended the call, unable to bear the weight of potentially disappointing her or sharing such dreadful news.

* * *

It was June 6th, the day my twin brother and I always celebrated our birthday. We were together, enjoying the special day when, out of nowhere, my aunt's voice broke through. She had news: Dr. Mohamed had carefully examined all my medical records and test results. But what was astonishing was that he didn't just agree to meet with me, he was eager to discuss the possibility of surgery. It felt like the most incredible and treasured birthday gift I could ever receive.

I turned to my twin brother and Kenneth, my eyes filled with a mix of happiness and tears said, "There's hope, Ken! Tomorrow morning, I'm meeting with the doctor to discuss all the details of the surgery. It seems like he's leaning towards going ahead with it." Our birthday celebration included Audi, Audi's fiance, my mother, my son, and, of course, Kenneth. Audi tried to keep the atmosphere light by cracking jokes, even though we all knew that a storm was coming.

The surgery was planned for just a week after my birthday. But before that, I had to meet with Dr. Mohamed to figure out all the details. There were still more tests and analyses to be done during the week before the surgery. We weren't sure yet about the neurosurgeon's role in all of this.

As each day passed, we got closer to the important surgery that would decide how I could fight the tumor.

Finally, the day came when I would see Dr. Mohamed. I was full of anticipation and nervousness as Kenneth and I walked into his office. We were hoping for some good news. The room felt very professional and Dr. Mohamed welcomed us with a warm smile.

"Good afternoon, Mrs. Rachel," Dr. Mohamed greeted, shaking my hand. "I've looked at your case, and I think we can help a lot with surgery. But we have to be really careful and get everything ready."

I agreed, feeling thankful and hopeful. "Thank you, Dr. Mohamed. I'm ready to do whatever it takes to beat this tumor and get better."

Dr. Mohamed talked about how the surgery would work, telling us about the possible problems and how we'd have to plan everything very carefully. He used sayings like "leave no stone unturned" to explain that we needed to be very precise, work together as a team, and stay determined.

"Don't worry," Dr. Mohamed said. "I've put together a team of really skilled professionals who will be with you the whole way. We'll face this challenge together."

The week leading up to the surgery was a whirlwind of medical tests, consultations, and final preparations. Each day brought a mix of anxiety and determination as we ticked off the items on our checklist. The neurosurgeon's involvement was seamlessly coordinated, aligning with Dr. Mohamed's vision of a well-executed surgical plan.

As the day of the operation drew near, emotions ran high. The support of my family and friends became an anchor, providing the strength and encouragement needed to face the unknown. The fear of the surgery was overshadowed by the prospect of reclaiming my health and embracing a future free from the clutches of the tumor.

Before the surgery, despite the considerable time that had passed since I last stepped into a church, my son and I were invited by my dear friend Sido to gather within those hallowed walls. With a sense of reverence and anticipation, we assembled to hold a powerful prayer to God.

Sido's unwavering confidence resonated in her words as she reassured me, "When we all come together in prayer, our collective faith becomes a guiding light to God." Her voice carried a conviction that enveloped us, urging us to immerse ourselves and our loved ones in a sacred, divine embrace."

As we stood together, Sido placed a hand on my shoulder and looked into my eyes, her gaze steady and reassuring. "Rachel, I want you to feel yourself and your family surrounded by sacred divinity," she said with a soft smile. "Leave every worry at his feet, and let Jesus find his place in your heart."

I nodded, my gratitude evident in my eyes. "Thank you, Sido. Your faith gives me strength," I replied, my voice tinged with emotion.

She squeezed my shoulder gently. "You've always had a strong faith within you, Rachel. Sometimes, life just nudges us to remember it."

With a shared understanding, we bowed our heads in unity, joining our hearts and intentions in prayer. As the prayers and hymns filled the air, I felt a wave of serenity wash over me. At that moment, amidst the soft whispers of devotion, Sido's words lingered in my mind, reminding me that this gathering was more than just a ritual—it was a conduit for our faith to unite, to connect us with the divine presence we sought.

In the quiet church, Sido spoke again, leading us in heartfelt prayer. "Rachel, let God's love surround you and your son, let it take away your fears."

As we kept on praying with our eyes closed and our hearts full, I felt something special. It was like the church's walls held a kind of power, a strong belief that went along with each word we said. Sido's voice and words were like a bridge that connected our worries with God's endless care.

In those moments, as Sido's voice faded into a gentle silence, I didn't need to open my eyes to know that God was there. His presence was palpable, like a warm embrace that cocooned us in love and hope. I opened my eyes, and there, amidst the holy ambiance, Sido smiled at me. It was a smile that held the depth of our shared faith, our unbreakable friendship, and the hope that transcended any words spoken or unspoken.

* * *

I remember the day before the surgery like it was happening right now. Those memories are so clear, each one full of feelings that were strange but very real. It all started with a special drink that was like medicine. I had to drink it to clean my body before the surgery. This was a huge challenge, especially because I couldn't eat anything, and the drink was so bitter and gross. I think it was called chlorhexidine. It smelled and tasted really bad. The bathroom became my safe place. I kept going there over and over, like a dance of needing to go and feeling better

On the day before the tide of change would sweep me into the operating room, I was in the company of my son. We wove moments together like threads of laughter, our currency of joy echoing through the house. Our laughter resonated, a shared secret binding us, and I found myself embracing him with a fierce tenderness. My arms, like protective fortresses, shielded him from the torrent of emotions that cascaded down my cheeks, each drop a testament to the love and uncertainty that coursed through me.

As morning came, I faced what was ahead. My little one's innocent voice rang in my heart as he said goodbye.

"Goodbye, Mommy," he said with a sweet tone that comforted my hurting heart.

I replied softly, trying to smile despite the trembling in my voice.

"I'll be back very soon," I promised, feeling a mix of longing and worry in my words.

I hoped I'd get better quickly and come back soon. But deep down, I knew this surgery was very tricky. Was I scared? Very, especially for my son. I couldn't bear the thought of leaving him all alone. I wanted to be there for him every step of the way – to comfort him when he got sick, to see his first day at school, to cheer for him at his graduation, to celebrate his wedding, and to be with him when he found love. These moments meant so much that the pain I felt was like my heart might burst. I held back my tears, keeping them hidden deep inside. In the car, I looked out of the window. I saw the world passing by, the busy streets, and the tall buildings. People rushing by with so much work to do. But, my friend, I urge you to pause, take a moment, and enjoy life's precious moments before they slip away forever.

Without even noticing it, we were already at the hospital. We had a suitcase with the things I might need. The air was thick with anticipation. Inside the hospital's clean walls, the doctor spoke in a very professional way, hiding the many feelings underneath.

He said, "We need to do one last MRI," making it sound like he was an artist about to create something amazing on a canvas.

My hospital room was like a sanctuary, but it also felt a bit scary. I turned to Kenneth and tried to look strong, hoping it would give us both courage.

"Don't worry, my love," I said, smiling, even though I felt really vulnerable inside. Kenneth looked at me with unwavering faith and responded with a strong belief.

"Yes," he whispered, showing his unshakable conviction. "We are in the hands of the best."

Even a nurse, who had caused us some trouble before, now seemed ironic. She jokingly called the room the "doctor's private enclave." Her tone was a mix of sarcasm and playfulness. Amid all these contradictions, I turned to Kenneth and spoke softly, as if I was sharing a secret with the universe.

"Yes, it's a privilege," I said softly, "to find ourselves in this sterile room, about to undergo a serious procedure."

Kenneth left for a moment, and another nurse arrived, indicating it was time for me to prepare for the upcoming procedure. I looked down the hallway, hoping to see Kenneth, but he was nowhere to be found. I started this journey without the usual goodbye as if the pages of parting were still unwritten or uncertain.

Walking down that corridor felt like walking along a bright path as if it were guiding my way. Putting on the hospital clothes, I felt an unusual calmness, like an invisible friend was with me. It was as if this friend walked beside me, whispering comforting words. "Don't be afraid," the voice seemed to say, soothing my worries. "Trust me, I'm here to help you carry your burdens. Let go of your fears, and I'll bear the weight for you."

This feeling was deep and comforting, a mix of happiness and relief that created a vivid picture of a divine presence. I felt cradled, held by a presence beyond understanding, perhaps an angel or even something divine itself.

As I lay down on the bed, the room felt strangely quiet and surreal. A practitioner, who looked a bit nervous, tried to give me a sedative to help me fall asleep.

"Ouch," I whispered, trying to hide the pain I felt.

The doctor, who was a professional, took over and explained things in a reassuring way. "Don't worry," he said, speaking with a soothing tone that seemed to calm the whole room like a gentle breeze.

Talking to the nurse, the doctor's assistant stated "Why is she still vested in her attire?"

After that, my memory gets hazy. Everything suddenly became so quiet, like a warm blanket covering my thoughts. I felt like I was floating in a peaceful place, connected to a world of calmness. Soft voices guided me through a mysterious land that lay ahead.

I couldn't tell if I was dreaming or awake, and my mind felt foggy, with moments of clarity in between.

I was starting to understand that the room was filled with loud voices. In the dim light, I caught a glimpse of my father, but Kenneth wasn't there. I called for him, my voice trembling, aching with pain that was too deep for words.

I was stuck between being aware and half-asleep, but I could sense something or someone touching me as if they were trying to rouse me from my drowsy state.

With all my strength, I fought to open my heavy eyes, desperate for some clarity. Time felt like a blur, but I knew I had survived the four-hour surgery. Still, I had no idea if my legs would move, silently praying deep inside.

After I saw myself in a smaller, cozier room with just one other patient. Kenneth, my rock, was right by my side, offering constant comfort. My brother, Audi, remained a steady source of support, always there for me. They never left me alone during this tough journey.

When I was feeling a little bit more conscious, fear rushed through as I realized I had two uncomfortable tubes in me. One was in my nose, and the other in my throat. The pain was intense; every breath hurt. I looked into the worried faces of Flora, Kevin, and Henri. They were all there, supporting me.

Kevin spoke softly, "Don't talk, just focus on getting your strength back."

Later, because of the strong medicine smell from the surgery, Kevin got sick and had to leave. Henri had the same issue. Only Flora, Kenneth, and Audi were able to stay with me. The room started to look different, getting smaller. The walls moved a little, and their shapes became clearer. Breathing was hard like I couldn't get enough air.

They got really scared and yelled, "Nurse! Nurse!"

A nurse came quickly with oxygen. Their faces showed they were worried about me. I felt bad for making them worry, but their love was so strong. After that, they were asked to leave so, I could rest and get better. I'll never forget that you were there with me, supporting me through it all.

The journey was really tough, with moments when the pain felt unbearable, and everything felt uncertain. But through it all, Kenneth was there, standing like a steady force in the middle of a storm. His constant care and presence gave me the strength to face each challenge. And even though the room felt small and suffocating, I was so grateful for all the love and support around me.

Amidst the tough times, there came a little spark of hope. Nurses and doctors worked really hard to make my pain better, changing medicines and watching how I was doing. Their know-how and kindness felt like a guiding light when things were really tough. Slowly but surely, the pain started to go away, and my breathing became easier. It was like the room got bigger somehow, letting me take good, deep breaths once more.

When I was able and ready to feel my body, I saw the wound. The wound was huge, starting from my chest and extending down to my pelvis. I was scared and terrified to take a look at it. Shocked, I found myself wondering why they had to make such a large incision, splitting my body in half. Tears welled up in my eyes.

Trembling, Yet I was alive, I could move my legs, I could breathe from now on, I carried within me a renewed sense of purpose, grateful for the precious gift of life.

The first three days were a nightmare. The pain was unbearable, and I couldn't move an inch without feeling like I was being ripped apart. Audi, my brother, was there, trying to keep my spirits up midst the agony.

"Hey sis, I brought you some water," Audi said, holding a cup up to my lips. "Gotta stay hydrated, you know?"

I managed a weak smile, my voice barely a whisper. "Thanks, Audi. You always know how to make me smile, even in the worst of times."

He chuckled softly. "Well, what are brothers for, right? Gotta keep you entertained in this glamorous hospital life."

The wound care was the worst part. Each time the medical team came to change the dressings, I braced myself for the searing pain that would follow. Tears flowed uncontrollably as they gingerly tended to the wound, but I refused to let the pain break me.

"It's going to be okay, Rachel," one of the nurses assured me. "Just a little longer, and you'll start feeling better."

I nodded, grinding my teeth. "I understand, but it hurts a lot."

Later that night, I think I was dreaming. The hospital room looked dim and eerie, with a sickly light that made long shadows on the walls, like creepy ghosts. The air was cold and uncomfortable, making every breath feel unwelcome. The walls, which were once white, had turned an unhealthy color as if soaking up the pain and sadness of many patients. Heavy curtains covered the windows, making the room seem permanently dark, with no way out. A flickering light above made a spooky buzzing sound and created an eerie glow that danced across the room.

Stepping into the hallway (oddly, I could walk), I was overwhelmed by a terrifying feeling. The floor made eerie noises, like it was hiding dark secrets, and the walls looked old and worn as if they remembered painful screams. The corridor stretched on and on, and the lights flickered like weak heartbeats. The air had a strange smell, a mix of medicine and decay that sent chills down my spine. In every corner, it felt like something was lurking, just out of sight, ready to jump out of the shadows. Faint footsteps in the distance seemed to be accompanied by whispers, forming a spooky choir. Each step was like a journey into a horrifying world, where reality mixed with nightmares, and the line between life and death faded.

Terrified by the horrifying vision, I opened my eyes to break free from its grasp. Yet, right beside me, there was something I thought I'd forgotten – a figure, the shadowy man. But this time, he wasn't by the door; he was close, right next to my bed. His icy breath and hollow eyes bore into me. The room seemed to shrink as his presence filled the air, suffocating me. His gaze pierced my soul. I tried to turn away, to escape his relentless stare, but it was as if his eyes had me trapped. Fear gripped my heart, making it hard to breathe.

Suddenly, a thought crossed my mind – that shadows fear the light. I remembered some verses from the Bible and recited them aloud to shield myself from the darkness.

"Even though I walk through the valley of the shadow of death, I will fear no evil, for you are with me; your rod and your staff, they comfort me." (Psalm 23:1-4) "Finally, my brethren, be strong in the Lord and in the power of his might. Put on the whole armor of God, that you may be able to stand against the wiles of the devil." (Ephesians 6:10-11)

Ultimately, I summoned my courage, inspired by scenes from my favorite show, "Charmed." I commanded with determination, "I

command you to depart, unclean spirit, in the name of Jesus Christ!"
(Mark 5:8).

To my shock, the creepy shadow vanished, as if it had evaporated into
nothing. Instead, I was now sharing a stare-down with the person in
the same room with me. She was looking at me with a mix of interest
and confusion in her eyes. It felt like she doubted my sanity. I was left
standing there, feeling lost, not sure about who I was anymore. That
encounter had shaken my sense of reality and self.

* * *

On the third day, they wanted me to start walking. I didn't really want
to because I was scared of how much it might hurt, but they said it was
important for my recovery.

The doctor said, "You can do it, Rachel. Just take one step at a time."

I was hesitant and really scared. I said, "I'm not sure if I can. The pain
is too much."

Audi, always good at motivating, said, "Come on, sis. You've faced
tougher challenges before. I believe in you."

With Audi on one side and the doctor on the other, I found the courage
to get out of bed. When I tried to take my first step, I got really dizzy,
and it felt like I might fall.

"I…I can't…breathe," I gasped, desperately clutching Audi's arm for
support.

The doctor's voice was filled with concern. "Easy now, Rachel. Take deep breaths. We'll go slow."

Eventually, I regained my composure and managed to take a few tentative steps. Each movement was accompanied by a mix of pain and relief.

The following day, I triumphantly made it to the bathroom. Audi couldn't resist injecting some humor into the situation.

"Well, sis, you've always wanted an entourage. Looks like I'm your personal bathroom attendant now."

I laughed weakly, grateful for his lightheartedness. "Thanks, Audi. I appreciate you being here for me, even in these not-so-glamorous moments."

As the days passed, I continued to push myself, taking more steps with each passing day. The journey was agonizing, but the progress was undeniable. Finally, after what felt like an eternity, the doctor gave me the green light for my discharge.

Before I could leave, I had to remove the stitches holding my wound together. Well, some of them. This wound wasn't ordinary; it was like a deep gap in my body. It started at my stomach and went all the way down to my core. It showed the battle that happened during surgery. The upcoming challenge felt like a ghostly presence, making me shiver with nervousness. I clenched my teeth tightly, biting my trembling lower lip.

As I lay on the hard bed, I prepared myself for what was about to happen.

The nurse, someone I feared and hoped for at the same time, began his serious task. The first pull brought a mix of feelings, like a surge of discomfort running through my nerves.

I tried to stay strong, but I couldn't help saying, "Ouch, ouch!" The room felt like it was closing in on me, a combination of waiting and pain, while sweat formed a shiny layer on my forehead.

Minutes felt like they were dragging on forever, with every stitch removal getting me closer to feeling free. There was a lot of discomfort, like a big orchestra of pain playing in my body. I shivered each time a stitch was taken out, feeling both hurt and relief at the same time, like a complicated and detailed pattern of sensations.

At last, when the last thread of the first part was removed, the nurse said, "You can get up now."

Getting out of bed, I felt so much lighter and free. The room seemed to get bigger, and the air felt easier to breathe like the walls were exhaling with me.

As we reached the car parked outside, the scorching weather made me incredibly uncomfortable. I started to feel weak and grew really anxious. I struggled to share my feelings with Kenneth, even though my breaths were shallow and desperate.

"I… can't… breathe," I wheezed, my voice trembling.

Kenneth didn't seem to grasp how much I was suffering. He kept pushing me to keep moving forward. Just when I felt I might collapse, a stranger intervened, sounding quite angry.

"Can't you see? She's about to faint! Get her inside, right now!"

I felt a wave of relief as I was ushered into an air-conditioned room, which helped me recuperate from the brutal heat. After a brief pause, we began our slow journey back home, with the car moving extra cautiously.

During the drive, numerous questions swarmed my mind. Was this the end, or perhaps just the beginning? In ten days, we'd finally learn the true nature of the mass from the biopsy. What if it's cancer? What steps should I take then? But I tried to reassure myself, thinking it was probably benign, similar to my mom's experience. Nonetheless, deep down, doubts lingered. These were just my hopeful thoughts, not certainties.

Five

Chapter 5

When I got back home from the hospital, I felt a wave of relief seeing my family and the cozy atmosphere. Our spacious and clean bathroom was a welcome change from the small, unwelcoming one at the hospital. My dear mother suggested I freshen up, and as I saw myself in the mirror for the first time since everything happened, I noticed my thick and wild hair, which seemed to have grown even more during my stay. I used my fingers to push a few strands away from my face. After taking a moment to rest, I planned to try washing my hair or get my family to help me with it. Being back home was a feeling I can't even describe; I was so grateful. I asked my mother how she had been, how my son was doing, and if he'd been keeping her busy. I also asked about her daily routine. I just kept talking, enjoying the comfort of being back home.

My mother helped me get comfy on the couch, arranging lots of pillows. She looked happy to see me, with a comforting smile on her face. She reminded me to focus on getting better.

"You're here, my dear. It warms my heart to see you," she said with affection in her voice. "Just concentrate on getting better. Don't let any worries trouble your mind."

"Rachel, I've made you a light soup with just bone broth to help you regain your strength. After spending ten days at the hospital, you've weakened because you couldn't eat," Mom said, sounding concerned.

"Well, they didn't let me eat real food there, just medications and fluids," I replied. "But now the doctor said I can have thicker soups. My temperature hasn't dropped below 100.4 degrees Fahrenheit yet. I still need to take antibiotics to prevent infection from the surgical wound. Everything will be okay; I just need to give myself some time," I added.

"Yes," she nodded, briefly lowering her head. Liam was in the kitchen, playing with his toys and running around, happy that Mom was there with him. I had missed him so much, and he had been my source of comfort and light.

While we were talking, I noticed my brother smoking a cigarette out on the balcony. The smoke from his cigarette swirled and got carried away by the wind. He was leaning against the balcony railing, lost in his thoughts and gazing into the distance.

"Hey, come inside. Smoking isn't good for you," I called out to him. He looked over, nodded, but took one last puff before putting out the cigarette.

"Yeah, you're right. Just needed a moment," he said, his voice sounding a bit tired. He came inside, and having him there made me feel both comfortable and cared for. It was nice to have my family around and feel at ease.

I turned to Audi with a weak smile and said, "I need your help to wash my hair because it smells really bad, and I can't stand it anymore."

Audi grinned and playfully ruffled his hair. "Of course, sis. I'll make sure you feel fresh and smell like a meadow of flowers again."

Standing at the sink, my mom took up the pitcher, ready to pour the water over my hair. As the first droplets touched my scalp, it was like a shock to my senses, the coldness and the sensation of being trapped causing an involuntary hitch in my breath. I tried to compose myself, telling myself it was just water, just a simple task, but the second cascade was even worse, a shiver coursing through me as if my body rebelled against this intrusion.

Out of nowhere, I let out a scream, and it surprised me as much as anyone. My mom's eyes got wide, and she quickly stopped the water. I could see the apology in her eyes, but I was too overwhelmed to say anything sensible. It wasn't her fault, but a mix of frustration and vulnerability had built up inside me.

"Rachel, are you okay? Did I hurt you?" she asked, her voice full of concern and guilt. I wanted to reassure her, to say it was just a reflex, but the words got stuck in my throat.

Audi, who's always paying attention, came in next. He had a playful grin at first, but he hesitated when he felt the tense mood. As he got closer, he seemed like he wanted to lighten things up and had a chuckle ready. But when I looked at him, all the irritation I was feeling spilled out, and my tone unintentionally sounded sharp.

"Go ahead, then," I replied, a bit of bitterness in my words. I didn't mean to be rude, but the frustration from earlier came out in my voice, mixing with my embarrassment and feeling of helplessness.

Audi's smile disappeared, and he looked surprised and understanding. He held the pitcher carefully, and the water sparkled in the light. But when the first drops touched me, my body reacted again, and he let out a shaky laugh, maybe to deal with my unexpected outburst.

For a moment, his laughter hung there, in contrast to the storm of emotions inside me. I felt angry, not at him, but at myself for not being able to do such a simple thing. I started feeling sorry for myself, a harsh reminder of how vulnerable I was.

I turned away, tears welling up in my eyes, and clenched my fists, my frustration turning into physical tension. It hit me hard – I couldn't even wash my hair without help. It felt like a blow to my independence, hurting like a thousand cuts.

As my family looked at each other with worry, I tried to get a grip on my emotions. It wasn't their fault, none of this was. But at that moment, I couldn't help but feel the burden of my limitations, and the road ahead seemed even harder than before.

"Rachel," Mom's voice was gentle, and she put her hand on my shoulder. "It's okay, dear. We're here to help you. You don't have to do it all on your own."

I sighed, feeling a bit of tension ease as I leaned into her touch. "I know, Mom. It's just frustrating."

Audi cleared his throat, his earlier playful mood now replaced with a sincere one. "Ray, remember that day at the lake when we were kids? You fell off the canoe, and I was scared you never wanted to go near water again."

I turned to him, a small smile forming on my lips. "Yeah, I remember. You jumped in after me and scared away the fish."

He grinned, his eyes twinkling. "Exactly. I might not have been the best lifeguard, but I've got your back."

Tears started to well up again, but this time, they were different. They were a mix of thankfulness and acceptance of the situation. My family, with all their imperfections, was my support during these tough times. We didn't need to say anything; we just understood each other with a look. In my vulnerability, I found strength in their constant support, and the difficult path ahead didn't seem as scary as before.

As the water kept running, washing not just my hair and face but also my tears, it felt like some of the weight I'd been carrying was being gently carried away.

That night, I laid down on the sofa, trying to find comfort despite the lingering pain. The familiar surroundings helped a bit, making me feel a little better. I was glad to rest in my place, but the ache from the day made it hard to feel at ease. I closed my eyes and eventually fell into a restless sleep.

But that peaceful feeling didn't last. During the quiet of the night, when everyone else was asleep, I suddenly heard my son crying in a way that made my heart ache. It was so distressing that without thinking, I tried to get up, only to feel a sharp pain shoot through my body, forcing me to lie back down immediately.

Kenneth's voice broke through the pain, a mix of worry and gentleness. "Rachel, stop. You need to rest. Let me check on him." He assured me that our son was with my mom and safe.

"Rachel, dear, you should lie down and rest," my husband said. His eyes were full of concern as he came closer. He reached out to lend a hand and make things easier for me.

I mustered a weak smile, grateful for his care. "Yeah, you're right. I just need a moment."

He nodded and stepped back to give me some space. With his help, I slowly eased back onto the sofa, even though it hurt. The cushions provided a bit of relief, which was nice. The room's familiar sights offered some comfort.

Tears welled up, and I found myself clenching my fists, torn between wanting to be with my son and facing my limitations. The pain was a stark reminder of what I couldn't do. At that moment, I felt defeated, like my body was working against me.

* * *

I had no idea that what I was going through, was just the start of a series of tough challenges that would test my strength and emotional stability. We were waiting to hear about the results of the test on the mass we'd sent to Italy, and not knowing was making me worried. My husband Kenneth was working hard to take care of our child and me, but our calm home was now filled with stress.

Having my mom around was a constant source of support during all this chaos. She had just spent a year recovering from her battles, yet here she was, taking care of me with a mother's love that was always there. Her warm smiles and gentle words were like a soothing balm for my pain, reminding me that even in the darkest times, there's still some light.

The nights felt never-ending, full of questions and a growing feeling of hurry. Every floorboard's creak seemed like it had a hidden message, and when Kenneth and the doctor talked in hushed tones, it left me curious. I'd gaze into the darkness outside, feeling an indescribable ache and a suspicion that something lurked there. The unknown filled the air, and as I tightened my fists, it wasn't just the pain motivating me – I was determined to uncover the truth, at any cost.

Chapter 6

I realized I was lucky to be able to walk and be with my loved ones, my family. But I kept asking myself every day, every minute, and every second: how long? How long would I be with them? Would I live long enough to see my son grow up and my parents grow old together? Why was the autopsy result taking so long? This question haunted me every moment.

Inside that house, I felt tired and trapped by the walls. So, despite the difficulty, I pushed myself to reach the coffee just outside the house.

After five days at home, I decided to take the first steps out of the door. I remember as it was happening today, that day was Saturday. Kenneth was holding me; I was in pain while pulling my body, trying to get out that door. I missed the routine so much – that routine that might seem empty to many of you. But for me, in those moments, it looked like paradise itself – the paradise I was eagerly awaiting—the air outside the walls of a house or a hospital. I hoped to go back to work, to feel tired and stressed again – to handle the daily pleasures and stresses.

Strange as it may sound, I missed that mundane yet crucial thing in human life. In my life, that monotony made me wake up every single morning!

The feeling of being outside, finally away from the walls of that medical prison, and feeling the light and warmth of the sun, made me draw a deep breath - a breath as if I was entering life for the first time. After going down the stairs, the pain my body felt in those moments didn't matter to me. It was a pain in which I found pleasure. There, in the yard, I felt the sun's warmth, caressing every cell of my body - a heat I allowed to melt every bone and every part of me. I realized how much I had missed that warmth and light. I could feel my hair shining even more, and my eyes looking so beautiful in the sunlight. I felt profound happiness, grateful that I was still there – in this world, that though difficult, tiresome, and often disappointing, allowed me to experience everything anew, once more. I was alive! That was the most important thing at that moment, I was alive!

It took us at least twenty minutes to get to the cafe next to the building. The pain was really strong, but my desire for something normal in Tirane pushed me to walk, even though it hurt a lot.

"Rachel, do you think you can make it all the way to the cafe?" Worried, Kenneth asked.

"I'm sure!" I said with confidence, showing my determination.

As we walked down a narrow street from the apartment building and reached the cafe on the other side, I couldn't help but notice people looking at me curiously, but it didn't bother me.

"We made it!" I said, feeling accomplished.

Kenneth leaned back in his chair, his dark hair falling over his forehead. "You know, this place has the best coffee in town," he said.

Audi, puffing on a cigarette in the corner, added with a smirk, "Yeah, but I still think my homemade brew gives it a run for its money."

I laughed. "Well, today I'm testing that claim."

Sitting in a plastic chair, I ordered, "Just a regular espresso, please."

Kenneth looked at me with a playful grin. "Are you sure you don't want to try something a bit fancier?"

I shook my head, my face determined. "Nope, keeping it simple today."

Audi raised an eyebrow, smoke coming from his lips. "Simple and determined, I like that."

While we waited for our orders, I looked around and enjoyed the natural surroundings. "You know," I thought out loud, "there's something special about being outside and having a cup of coffee."

Kenneth agreed, "Absolutely. It's a small break from the daily routine."

Audi tapped the ashes off his cigarette, "And a moment to just be here, without any worries."

I smiled, the pain from my wound briefly forgotten. "Exactly. It's like time slows down for a little while."

Our coffee arrived, and I took a sip of my espresso. I closed my eyes, savoring the flavor.

Kenneth lifted his cup for a toast, "To enjoying life's simple pleasures."

Audi chuckled, "And to Rachel's unstoppable spirit."

As we clinked our cups together, I felt a sense of togetherness. Despite the pain and challenges, being in this moment with my family made it all worth it.

After we finished our coffee, we settled on the cozy balcony of the house, like secret watchers of the world below. Down in the yard, something interesting was happening that caught our attention – Liam, a bundle of endless energy, was playing with his friends. It was like a colorful whirlwind of childhood, and Liam was in the middle of it all.

"Hey, look at this!" I gently elbowed my mom and pointed to Liam. "He's trying ballet with Ona!"

Liam's attempt at ballet was incredibly cute. Imagine a kid with little feet, bouncing around as if doing magic. It was like his feet were having their own party. And you know what? He was copying her moves like a dance team. It was a sight that was too precious for words.

But in the midst of all this cuteness, my emotions were a mess inside me. I was obsessed with being near Liam, even if he didn't realize it. It was like I had become something delicate, like an egg that could break easily. I might have been driving my mom a little crazy, always asking her to keep an eye on Liam, worried he might get into trouble or hurt. Did he eat? Did he sleep? These thoughts made me anxious, maybe because I just couldn't be close enough to him.

Every now and then, he'd give me a hug, but even that felt a little sad. His smell was comforting, but it somehow made everything hurt a bit more. Strangely, even though he was right there, it felt like he was slowly moving away from me. A heavy feeling of sadness took over, and I felt, well, really terrible. I was basically shutting out the world, not letting myself or anyone else in because something was wrong with me.

But something wasn't making sense to me, and my thoughts were spinning, stuck on the mysterious situation with the biopsy results. Then, later in the afternoon, a surprise twist - Kenneth's phone buzzed, a message from the hospital lighting up the screen. The biopsy results had arrived, and they wanted him to come to the doctor's office first thing in the morning. Now, I'd been brewing a storm of suspicion for a while, convinced that some terrible secret was being kept from me. So, you can be sure that I was determined to go with him the next day.

Here comes the big showdown! We faced off in a battle of wills, with Kenneth coming up with excuses as fast as a rabbit running from a fox, just to keep me from coming along. But I was wearing my stubborn hat, insisting that I had the right to know what was in store for me.

And there he was, sitting in a corner of the couch, lost in his thoughts. I mustered up my courage, preparing for the worst. Inhale, exhale – I steadied myself and, taking a leap of faith, decided to speak up, my voice a bit louder, "Hey, enough with the cold vibes! Trust me, the story's already written. No need to lose sleep over it!"

The next morning came, and I was ready to face whatever the doctor had to say. The neurosurgeon held the answers we needed. Kenneth parked the car right outside our apartment and helped me as I carefully got in. A heavy silence filled the car during the short drive to the hospital, just two minutes away. We arrived, and I looked at the intimidating flight of stairs since there was no elevator. But I wasn't about to give up; not then, not ever. I pushed myself, determined to push my limits. Even if I felt like I might faint, it didn't matter – the truth was all that mattered.

So, with shallow breaths, we found ourselves in front of the doctor's office. Kenneth looked at me, a mix of concern and an attempt to hide his own worries. I knew him very well, better than anyone else. He was good at hiding his feelings, but in the end, I could always figure out what he really felt.

"Please, come in," the doctor called to us. "Have a seat," he gestured.

I remember it clearly - the doctor's face showed surprise, and he looked puzzled. Why was I there? I shouldn't be, not at that moment. He chose his words carefully like he was talking in a secret code with Kenneth. Then, after a short pause, he lowered his head and said, "As we expected, the answer is what we talked about. This confirmation helps us decide what to do next." The words hung in the air, heavy, and I seemed to be the only one who felt it."

The doctor's gaze shifted, his eyes meeting mine for a fleeting moment, a silent message passing between us. His lips formed a half-smile, a mix of understanding and shared concern. I wasn't sure exactly what he was talking about, but the gravity of his words was undeniable.

Quickly, Kenneth jumped in, thanking the doctor and sounding like there was a need for speed. "We'll contact you soon to talk about what comes next," he said firmly. I managed to smile, even though it felt very delicate, and I tried to compose myself.

As we walked down the hall, I couldn't help but have a lot of questions.

"What does that mean?" I asked, sounding worried.

Kenneth paused for a moment, looking to reassure me. "You're fine. We'll start radiation therapy in about a month, and we'll meet the doctor who will explain everything then."

"But if I'm fine, why do I need radiation therapy?" I questioned, feeling a knot of worry in my stomach. "I've already had surgery. If the results are really normal and not malignant cancer, why do I need this therapy? It doesn't make sense. Are you telling me everything, or is there something else going on that I don't know about?"

He looked into my eyes, his gaze steady and comforting. "The doctors want to make sure they get rid of every bit of the cancer and all the cells near the wound," he explained. "That's why they're suggesting this treatment." His words were meant to make me feel better, but I couldn't help but feel unsure.

I tried to read his eyes, to see if there was more to what he was saying, but it was like trying to understand a secret code or solve a puzzle with missing pieces. Despite his reassurance, I couldn't shake the feeling of uncertainty. It was like a persistent itch in my mind. I really wanted to trust him and believe in the plan, but the uncertainty kept nagging at me, like a quiet voice in the back of my head. In that moment, I wished I could see into his thoughts through his eyes, to know the real truth behind his words.

But there we stood, suspended in a moment where words hung heavy, where emotions and unspoken questions hovered like a mist between us. He was a fortress, his face revealing nothing, leaving me to wonder if my doubts were merely shadows or something more tangible. The room felt charged, not with anger or frustration, but with the electric pulse of uncertainty.

I knew one thing for sure – whether or not I understood every detail, I had to believe that every decision being made was in my best interest. Still, the desire to see beyond his composed exterior, to glimpse even a fraction of what lay beneath, lingered like an unsolved riddle.

Seven

Chapter 7

My fever had finally gone away, and I felt much better. I used to be very weak and couldn't even get out of bed, but now I could walk and move around easily. After two months, I started taking care of my son again. Finally, I went back to work after a week. I had to be careful not to push myself too hard.

I remember the day when the receptionist called and suggested a helpful idea. They decided to help me with the interviews, so I wouldn't have to go up and down the stairs, which I couldn't do yet. They would take each candidate to the second floor for the interviews, where I could be comfortable. I was really thankful for how understanding and caring my colleagues were. Just going to the second floor felt like a big accomplishment and a step toward getting back to normal after my illness.

I got back to work with a new sense of purpose. I felt really good when I completed my tasks and helped my team. Each task I finished and every meeting I went to showed how strong I was becoming. I was still careful because my body was still getting better, but I couldn't help feeling proud of what I was achieving. The problems I faced before were starting to turn into steps towards a better future.

The next day, I felt a mix of excitement and nervousness as I got ready to meet the doctor who would help me with the next part of my recovery: radiation therapy. This appointment was a big step, like a bridge between what I'd been through and what was coming next. I had a lot of different feelings about this new phase - hope, worry, and determination all mixed together.

When I look back, I see the tough weeks, the determination, and the constant support from my loved ones that got me here. The journey wasn't finished, but as I stood at this turning point, I couldn't help but recognize the strength I found in myself.

I was outside the hospital, talking to the receptionist. Her busy desk was like a small world of the hospital's activity. There was an exciting feeling in the air, mixed with the quiet talks between other patients waiting nearby. The waiting room was like a painting, showing all the feelings of the people there - hope, worry, and determination.

The receptionist broke the tension by saying, "Good afternoon, how can I help you today?" I answered, "Hello, I have an appointment with Dr. Ryan. I'm here to talk about radiation therapy." She was kind and professional, saying, "Of course, let me check you in. Can you fill out this form while you wait?"

I found myself among all the people waiting. The seriousness of the situation felt heavy on my shoulders. Each chair held someone looking for relief, each with their own story in their eyes. People were talking quietly, turning pages and a clock was ticking, making a peaceful and soothing sound.

An old man let out a gentle sigh and said, "These waiting rooms, seem to hold time in a tight grip, don't they?"

I smiled, agreeing with him, "Yes, they do make time feel like it's stretching. It can be quite nerve-wracking, right?"

He nodded and said, "Very nerve-wracking. But in these rooms, we realize that our journeys, no matter what they are, connect us."

I nodded back and added, "Speaking of that, would you like my seat? You've been waiting for a while."

He looked surprised, with grateful and amazed eyes, "Your kindness warms my heart, young one. Thank you. Small acts mean a lot."

In a sudden, emotional twist, a familiar face emerged from the bustling crowd – Lela, adorned in a pristine white coat. It struck me like a lightning bolt; she was one of the physicians here. Concern etched deep lines across her face, and she greeted me with a heartfelt, "Well, well, what a surprise! How have you been?"

A wry, bittersweet grin graced my lips, and I replied, my voice tinged with genuine astonishment, "The feeling's mutual! I certainly didn't expect our paths to cross here. I'm here to consult with Dr. Ryan."

Lela's laughter seemed to dance through the air, an acknowledgment of the serendipity of our encounter. After a brief consultation with the doctor's office, she returned, her curiosity evident, "So, spill the beans.

What brings you to Dr. Ryan?"

The weight of my circumstances bore down on me as I exhaled slowly, the words heavy with emotion, "Life has thrown me a few curve balls lately, and it appears that radiation therapy is the next chapter." Lela's empathetic response served as a soothing balm to my worries, "I'm truly sorry to hear that, but I deeply admire your proactive steps. Remember, I'm here to provide support whenever you need it."

As I walked into the doctor's office, I noticed a man who seemed friendly and confident. Dr. Ryan had kind, blue eyes that made me feel like he knew a lot and could help me. He didn't look very special, with sandy blond hair and a regular body, but there was something about him that made me feel comfortable.

Dr. Ryan greeted me with a smile that made me feel less nervous. He said, "Good afternoon. I'm Dr. Ryan. How do you feel about the radiation therapy that's coming up?"

I couldn't hide my worry and said, "I have to admit, I'm pretty anxious. This is something new."

Dr. Ryan explained all the details about the therapy, like how long it would take and how often I'd have to go (two weeks, five days a week, in the morning). He also talked about the possible risks, like how close the treatment would be to my reproductive organs and what that might mean for my ability to have kids in the future. He was honest and understanding, knowing that this was a big decision—getting rid of any remaining bad cells from the surgery but maybe not being able to have children later.

The decision weighed on me like a heavy stone, and I felt uncertain. But it was the love I had for my son that gave me the strength I needed.

With a resolute heart, I signed the necessary paperwork, ready to embark on my radiation therapy journey.

As the appointed time drew near, the strangers who shared the waiting room with me began to feel like kindred spirits. We were bound by our shared anxieties and the hope of healing. The waiting room became a sanctuary where we could openly express our fears and dreams, finding solace in our shared humanity.

* * *

On the day of my first radiation treatment, I felt really embarrassed and vulnerable. I had misunderstood how it worked, and I was surprised to learn that I had to undress from my belly down. Two young boys were there to help me, and the difference between my vulnerability and their youthful innocence made the situation even more complicated.

The first boy was tall, with a sun-kissed complexion and muscles showing beneath his skin. The second boy was shorter, with a waterfall of black hair. They both had a youthful vibe, but for some reason, their youth made me even more uneasy. They tried to talk to me, maybe to ease the tension, but my nervousness stuck around despite their efforts.

The tall assistant broke the silence and asked a direct question that made me a bit uncomfortable, "Can you tell us where your injury is? We want to make sure we treat that area carefully. You'll need to lie face down and take off your pants so we can do the radiation accurately." He noticed my embarrassment and added kindly, "Please, don't be ashamed. This is our job, and we help every patient that needs us. Hospitals are for healing. Try to relax and stay very still. The procedure will take about thirty minutes, and it's really important that you don't move."

He reached out his hand to help me get onto the big machine nearby. It was a supportive gesture, but as I struggled with my pants, I felt a rush of self-consciousness. I felt so vulnerable at that moment like my dignity was clashing with what needed to be done.

The whole thing felt terrible like I had no choice but to go along with it. I had to summon my courage and resilience to face this unsettling ritual. I hoped that maybe, as time went on, this routine would become less uncomfortable, or at least, I'd grow more accustomed to it.

But despite all the awkwardness, I made a decision to go through with it. I climbed onto the cold surface of the big machine, knowing it was a crucial step toward healing.

As the procedure continued, it felt like time was stretching out, each moment etching itself into my memory. The machine hummed mechanically, and my heartbeat provided an unexpected rhythm amid my vulnerability. The young attendants, who had made me uneasy before, now became like guardians of this profound experience. Their professionalism created a shield against embarrassment, and I felt supported in their presence.

How about you? Yes, you. Have you ever faced a challenging situation that made you feel vulnerable but stronger in the end? Probably, you do too...

The time passed slowly, and each minute showed how strong I could be. The tall helper's voice was calm and comforting, guiding me through the process. His words, even though they were ordinary, felt like a lifeline when I was feeling self-conscious.

"Stay still, just a bit longer," he said, and I held onto those words like they were my anchor in rough waters.

As we got closer to the end, I felt a mix of relief and pride. I had faced my own insecurities and proved to myself that I could handle even the most uncomfortable situations. The big machine that did the radiation treatment stopped, and its role in my healing journey was done. The helpers made it easy for me to stand up, and their support was like an extension of the journey I had just been through.

Putting my clothes back on felt like a big moment. The fabric was like a shield, protecting me from the vulnerability I had just experienced. The young helpers exchanged a knowing smile, silently recognizing the emotional journey we had all been on, not just the physical one.

As I walked out of the room, the world seemed a bit brighter. The embarrassment I had felt had transformed into a symbol of strength. The hospital corridor, which used to be just a hallway, now echoed with my courage. Every step I took made me realize that being vulnerable doesn't mean you're weak. It's like a canvas where resilience paints its most vivid pictures.

Days went by, and each radiation session was like a new part of my healing story. The initial embarrassment started to fade, and I learned to accept it. The young helpers weren't just assistants; they were like partners in my journey. This journey wasn't only about my body getting better; it was also about becoming emotionally stronger.

Looking back, that first day of radiation meant more than just a hospital visit. It was a turning point, a step toward embracing vulnerability and facing discomfort directly. As the treatments went on, I found comfort not only in the promise of physical healing but also in the inner strength I gained.

I discovered that strength isn't just about conquering physical challenges; it's also about navigating the maze of feelings that often come with them. Every time I went for treatment, it was like a blank canvas for personal growth, a chance to change how I saw being vulnerable and redefine what it means to be strong.

As time passed, that first feeling of embarrassment started to go away. In its place, I found a beach covered in resilience, self-discovery, and the understanding that sometimes, our true strength comes from the most uncomfortable moments.

The last day of radiation therapy had finally arrived, bringing a glimmer of hope that played around in my thoughts. To mark this special day, I decided to celebrate with a small makeover. I let my blonde hair fall to my shoulders, which made me feel like a new person. A touch of mascara highlighted my eyes, and a lovely brown lipstick made my lips stand out, giving me a much-needed boost of confidence. This transformation was about more than just looks. It symbolized the end of a tough journey and the start of a new chapter.

As I stood before the mirror, a hint of a smile tugged at my lips. The reflection that stared back exuded strength, a testament to resilience that whispered of battles fought and endurance proven. The room seemed to bask in a soft glow, mirroring the warmth that radiated from within me. This was more than just the end of a treatment—it was a reclamation of normalcy, a rekindling of a life momentarily put on hold.

Filled with hope, I walked into the hospital, every step a mix of excitement and worry. Dr. Ryan welcomed us, and his experience put us at ease. He greeted me as if we were old friends, saying, "Hi, Rachel. How are you doing and feeling?" His words were filled with care, making me feel like I had support on this journey.

I couldn't help but smile, revealing the happiness welling up inside me. "I'm good, thank you. I'm really happy that this is my last therapy session." I felt a sense of joy and pride as I contemplated leaving behind the exhausting routine. My excitement shone in my eyes. Well, at least that's what I'm hoping for, the end of this suffering…

His response, however, was an unexpected shock that hit me like a wave. "Well, you should know, there's still one more challenge to face before it's all done." His words hung in the air, creating a sudden tension in the room. What did he mean? The joy I had just felt evaporated, replaced by a gnawing worry in my stomach.

Like every person in the room had many questions, so did I, and without knowing what would happen next. I was eager to understand this "challenge" and what would come after. The words felt like a distant storm, making the calmness tense.

Amid my thoughts, Kenneth's voice was like a comforting hug, calming my worry. He said, "Don't worry; everything will be alright," and it made me feel better. But my curiosity was still strong; I wanted to uncover what Dr. Ryan's mysterious message meant.

As time passed, I couldn't shake the feeling that finishing radiation therapy was just the start of something big and unknown. I had so many questions, like stars in the night sky. What was waiting for me? Was Kenneth hiding something? What wasn't he telling me? The answers felt just out of my grasp, hanging in the air.

Eight

Chapter 8

The next day, I posted a picture on Instagram with my new short haircut, captioning it as "New me." It was something I hadn't done much before, but I figured, why not embrace change? It can be refreshing.

Soon, comments began to pop up:

"Looking beautiful!"

"Absolutely gorgeous!"

Then came a comment from my friend Joanna: "Why did you decide to cut your hair so short? I loved your long hair!"

I responded with a simple, "Just felt like trying something different."

As the days passed, my first chemotherapy session was getting closer. It was almost November's first week, and we were preparing for some necessary blood tests. The doctor needed to understand my overall health condition before we could begin the first round of therapy. These blood tests were essential for a few reasons:

To establish a starting point for my blood counts and general health.

To customize the treatment plan based on these blood results.

To ensure safety throughout the treatment process.

To keep an eye on how my body responds to the treatment and spot any potential side effects.

The days were speeding by, and my first therapy session was getting closer by the minute. I knew that on the first day, I wouldn't be alone; my sister-in-law, Aria, would be there with me, offering her support. Aria had just completed nursing school, so she had a wealth of knowledge about many things. She was a tall, striking woman with long, beautiful blonde hair that gracefully flowed down, perfectly matching her captivating hazel eyes. Unfortunately, Kenneth couldn't come with me because of his work commitments. Someone had to earn a living, after all.

I approached the entrance, and as usual, there was a guard there, managing the flow of people entering, either two at a time or one by one. The scene that unfolded inside was enough to send shivers down anyone's spine, reminding us of the tough road ahead. After meeting with Dr. Nola, a knowledgeable and caring doctor, she led us to the room where my therapy would take place. When I stepped inside, the sight before me was undeniably gloomy. Rows of beds were closely arranged in a large, somber gray room. There were a few TVs scattered around, but there was hardly anything worth watching. The room was filled with both men and women who were all facing a common enemy—cancer. They looked incredibly frail and weak, and when it came to their hair—there wasn't any. They resembled ghostly figures, straddling the line between the living and the dead.

My sister-in-law was asked to assist with some simple tasks while waiting for me. Ha-ha, it all seems amusing to me now as I reflect, but at the time, they genuinely needed the help. She found joy in assisting however she could.

Once I settled into the bed, Ina, a young woman, approached me. She wore a comforting smile and said,

"Don't worry, we'll insert an IV into your arm, and you'll receive your medication through it. No need for multiple injections."

Oh, the dread I felt for needles, and here I was, succumbing to them, devoid of any alternative.

"Thank you," I stammered, my voice quivering.

I glanced at the needle, then turned my head and squeezed my eyes shut. "Ouch," I let out a little sound of pain, trying hard not to cry. I thought this was the easy part. The real challenge, the therapy itself, was still ahead of me. I wasn't sure how it would make me feel. I knew it might leave me tired and possibly queasy, but I couldn't predict for sure.

"Hello, I'm Laura," a voice from my right side broke in. She had drawn the curtain and struck up a conversation with me. Most of the time, I preferred not to talk about my condition, my feelings, or anything like that. I hesitated to share my emotions with anyone. I wanted to keep everything locked up inside, silent, and all to myself. That's where I found comfort.

"Hello," I responded curtly.

"You're quite young, and I love your hair," she said, seemingly aiming to reassure me.

"Um, thank you," I replied hesitantly.

As she looked at my wedding ring, she inquired further, "Do you have children?"

"Yes," I answered, silently pondering the number of offspring I had.

And there we were, embarking on the customary Albanian-style conversation upon meeting someone for the first time. I hated it, truly. I lacked the patience to engage in idle talk with anyone, anyone at all. Nonetheless, I was determined not to come across as uneducated.

"One," I responded.

"Only one? I have seven children. Oh, I had a blast when I was young. I'm ecstatic that I had the opportunity to raise them and witness their happiness and good health," she continued.

"Good for you," I replied, forcing a slight smile, my lips trembling, hiding my true emotions.

There I was, faking a smile and trying to hold on to the medicine that was making me feel tired. She was still continuing to talk about her grown-up children and her life.

"Oh, you know," she chuckled, "adult kids are like a box of chocolates.

You never know what you're gonna get, but you still love them all the same!"

I managed a weak smile, "Absolutely, the surprises just keep coming!"

"Yes, well, let me tell you about the time my youngest thought they were a culinary genius and attempted a five-course meal. Let's just say the fire department had to get involved."

I couldn't help but burst into laughter at that image. "Oh no, not the fire department! That's quite the ambitious chef."

She grinned, "Indeed! The kitchen was never the same after that, but it made for a memorable family dinner!"

As we shared more stories, the conversation lightened, and for a little while, I forgot about the IV and the reason I was there. Laughter truly is the best medicine, but my eyes were starting to close slightly.

And there I was, lying in bed, feeling like my eyes and my breath were being pulled down, down, as if I could let everything fall apart. Then, a cold touch on my left hand made me jolt with fear. I struggled to understand what it was. Suddenly, I saw that ominous figure again, way too close for comfort. It was a darkness deeper than the night, covering his eyes and face, making them disappear. In terror, I snapped my eyes open, hearing Ariel's urgent voice, "Rachel, Rachel, please wake up!"

Still haunted by the intense and terrifying dream, I fought to regain control over my body, but it felt unresponsive. I was like a heavyweight, unable to move, my limbs like dead weights. I felt utterly exhausted.

"Rachel, we're finished. It's time to head home. Come on, I'll help you," Ariel assured me, her words breaking through the fog of fear clouding my mind. They'd removed the IV from my left arm, but I hardly noticed. We were ready to leave. It took considerable effort, but I managed to sit up and, with her gentle guidance, we took small steps toward the exit.

As we left the hospital, darkness had already blanketed the world. I headed toward a waiting taxi, eager to return home. I gave the driver our address, and we arrived shortly thereafter. On my way home, my dependable son Liam was waiting for me, a source of comfort amidst the chaos. After changing out of my hospital clothes and into something more comfortable, I silently thanked a higher power for giving me another day to watch my child grow. Dinner had been thoughtfully prepared before my hospital visit, knowing I'd be weak. Kenneth would soon return from work, expecting a home-cooked meal. Unfortunately, I could only manage to eat a handful of sunflower seeds. My stomach was unsettled, a reminder of the torment I had been through.

"We're all home," I said, my voice filled with relief.

Kenneth, after returning from work, chimed in, "It's good to be back with my favorite people."

Ariel added with a smile, "And we missed you, Kenneth."

We all sat down, and Kenneth shared his day, trying to lighten the mood. "You won't believe what happened at work today."

I managed a laugh, "Tell us, I could use a distraction."

As the evening waned, exhaustion began to weigh on me. "I think I need some rest. It's been a long day."

Kenneth nodded understandingly, "Of course, love. Get some rest."

Ariel reassured, "We're right here if you need anything, Rachel."

With gratitude, I expressed, "Thank you, both of you. I appreciate it."

After some time, feeling drained, I went to my room. "Goodnight, everyone. I'll see you in the morning."

Kenneth wished, "Sleep well, my dear."

Ariel added warmly, "Sweet dreams, Rachel."

Drifting off to sleep, I felt the comfort of their presence, grateful for the love and care surrounding me.

* * *

The next day, I tried to find a bit of hope in my tired body, but the chemotherapy kept making me feel unwell. It was like a never-ending storm inside me, leaving me feeling seasick all the time, unable to eat. I used to have the strength to take care of my son, but it was slipping away, and I felt like I couldn't do enough for him.

With every passing moment, my burden got heavier, and I was filled with a mix of anger and worry. I was frustrated with my body for letting me down, angry at the constant sickness inside me, and anxious about how it was affecting not only me but also the people I loved.

But amid all the chaos and my tiredness, there was one small relief - my son going to his private preschool. It was a brief break, a little light in the middle of the storm that gave me some hope. He would be busy and well taken care of, giving me a few precious hours to rest and gather some energy, maybe even cook a good meal for him later.

Kenneth took our son to preschool. I watched them from the doorway, feeling a mix of emotions. I was proud of my son, ready to learn and grow. Grateful for Kenneth, always there to help and show love. But I also felt sad that I couldn't take him myself, and share that special moment.

As the door closed behind them, the house suddenly felt too quiet. The clock on the wall seemed louder than ever, ticking away in empty rooms. I sank into the couch, tiredness sinking into my bones. Breathing was hard, a reminder of the battle inside me.

I closed my eyes, trying to gather my strength. It took a lot of effort, to pull together every bit of resilience I had. I thought of my son, his smile, his laughter - they gave me the motivation. With a deep breath, I told myself, "I'll find the strength for him."

In that solitary moment, I realized that gathering strength wasn't just a physical act. It was about summoning the courage, the will, and the determination to keep going. To hold on, even when it seemed impossible. Slowly, I began to find that inner strength, that flicker of determination pushing me to endure and strive.

And so, in the quiet of my home, I began to gather my courage, thread by thread, weaving a resilience that would carry me through each challenging day. It was a journey, a battle fought within, but I was determined to emerge stronger, for myself and for the little one who depended on me.

After a moment of reflection, I remembered that I could asked Neta, an incredible person, and Kenneth's cousin's wife. She was always willing to lend a helping hand, to pick up Liam from preschool and bring him home. My weakness had reached a point where even this simple task seemed insurmountable.

I dialed Neta's number, my fingers moving slowly over the keypad. Each press felt like a weighted effort, but determination fueled my actions. "Hello, Neta," I greeted, my voice carrying the fatigue I felt.

"Hi there, how are you holding up?" Neta's caring tone instantly made me feel a bit lighter.

"I'm having a tough day. Can you pick up Liam from preschool? I just don't have the energy," I confessed, my words weighed down by a feeling of giving in.

"Of course, no problem. I'll go get him," she said, her words soothing my frayed nerves.

I felt so thankful. "Thank you, Neta. It means a lot to me."

"Anytime, Rachel. We're all here for you. Liam will be home soon," she reassured me.

After we hung up, I felt a mix of feelings - relief that Liam would be back soon, grateful for the support I had, and a hint of sadness that I couldn't be the one to pick him up.

* * *

After the third or fourth weeks of my first chemotherapy, something frightening happened. I was in a restless sleep, and my heart, usually steady like a metronome, started pounding in my chest like a wild storm. It wasn't just strong; it was all over the place, hurting with every beat.

"Rachel," he whispered, worry in his voice, "are you okay?"

I grabbed my chest, trying to catch my breath as the pain got worse. "I... I don't know. It's like my heart's going crazy."

Fear showed on Kenneth's face as he sat up, reaching for the phone. "We can't wait. I'm taking you to the hospital."

His urgency made me even more scared. Each thump of my heart felt like a heavy hammer against my ribs. We called his aunt so she could come take care of Liam.

"Kenneth, I'm so scared," I said in a trembling voice.

He gripped my hand firmly, offering me stability in the chaos. "We'll make it through this. Just stick with me."

Each minute felt like it stretched on forever as we hurried to the car, facing the unknown, the pain unrelenting and unforgiving. Kenneth tried to distract me, talking about our son, and our future plans, attempting to bring comfort in the face of fear.

"Just hang on, Rachel. We're getting you to the hospital," he assured me, his eyes showing his own worry.

As we raced towards the hospital, the city lights became streaks of color, reflecting the whirlwind of emotions inside me. I felt as though my heart was like a bird trapped in a cage, its wings fluttering incessantly, longing to break free from the inner turmoil.

"We're always in a hurry to get to the hospital," Kenneth exclaimed, his frustration evident in his voice.

I nodded, fully understanding his irritation. "I know, but we'll find a way. Let's concentrate on getting through this challenging night," I whispered, feeling my loneliness and desperation intensify.

"I knew he was becoming as tired of hospitals as I was, but I needed his support by my side. I couldn't help but feel that he was growing distant and exhausted from it all. 'Are you going to give up now?' I wondered to myself."

Nine

Chapter 9

I was still in the doctor's office, and time seemed to slow down. I looked at both of them, and we shared a silent understanding. In the quiet, I desperately wanted them to explain the mystery they mentioned and tell me what this new challenge was all about.

The doctor gazed at me, and he had a slight smile as he spoke with calm confidence, "You'll need chemotherapy, but it's only for four months. I talked to the head of the chemotherapy department about you. I told them how remarkable you are, which is why I've been so thorough and careful."

During those moments, I couldn't say a word, and I was deeply shocked. Chemotherapy? But why? Kenneth had said the biopsy was okay. So, why do I need chemotherapy? My mind was flooded with confusing thoughts that shattered the certainty I had built. Kenneth didn't say a word, but I was almost sure he was hiding something from me. None of this made sense.

"Kenneth, the director is over there. Please go to the building next door and fill out the paperwork," said Dr. Ryan.

"Sure thing, Doctor," Kenneth replied, showing that he understood and would follow the instructions.

After Kenneth thanked the doctor, we left the office. My eyes played tricks on me; the hallway seemed to disappear into darkness, with just a faint glow around the exit where we were headed. It took only two minutes to reach the other department. As I walked, it felt like my body wasn't really mine; I was just going through the motions on the way to chemotherapy.

We reached the main entrance. Kenneth gestured for me to sit at the reception desk. But could I actually bring myself to sit there? I looked around, taking in everything: sad, pale faces, everyone looking fragile. An invisible illness was silently taking lives, without any care. The chills down my spine were getting stronger and more persistent. In a corner, a young woman's eyes met mine, full of understanding. But the heartbreaking truth was that she held her children close. Please, God, protect them. Keep them safe. These kids were the guardians of innocence and pure light.

I struggled to breathe, got up from the chair, and mustered the strength to move toward a small courtyard. Even there, the air felt heavy and lifeless. Then, I saw Kenneth's face, a source of comfort from another world, guiding me forward. Okay, I can do this, keep moving. The guard had mentioned that only two people at a time could go inside, but Kenneth's gaze pulled me in, and we walked down another hallway. I saw him enter an office, holding a stack of papers. My vision had abandoned me. The oppressive, dark shadows refused to offer even a hint of visibility. It felt unbearable, and at that moment, I gave in. Leaning against the cold, white hospital wall, I slowly sank to the floor, my hands clutching my head. Tears streamed down my face, and I couldn't stop them. I was overwhelmed by confusion and disarray, making it hard to breathe, and I sobbed like a child, the sound echoing through the hallways. I had lost control.

Suddenly, I felt a soft hand on my shoulder, it seemed like it might be a woman's hand. What would happen next? The uncertainty hung in the air, making the moment even more intense.

"Let your tears flow. They can help ease the pain. Sorrow shouldn't be kept inside," a gentle voice broke through my daze, grounding and making me aware of the people around me.

Gathering every bit of strength, I lifted my head, tears blurring my view, and there she stood—a woman. Her eyes carried the weight of a mother's sadness, fixed on me. She looked to be in her fifties, nearly as tall as me. She appeared to be in decent health, with short, dark hair draping over her shoulders. Her eyes, the color of deep coffee, locked onto mine as if silently saying, "Be strong." In her other hand, she held an unopened water bottle, offering it to me.

"You need it more than I do right now. Yes, everything might seem dark but don't give up. Fight, fight with all your might. You're young, don't let it slip away," her words washed over me like a soothing melody, a comforting symphony. What would happen next, and how could her words guide me through this? The suspense hung in the air.

In the midst of the bustling crowd, Kenneth's voice pierces through the chaos.

"Rachel, come inside, they need you too!"

With trembling legs, I cautiously enter the room, my voice quaking as I manage to ask,

"How are you?"

"We need to make sure it's really you," they say, and we leave the room. It's like they wanted to be sure I was a real person like they had doubts about me. But we were there, part of a plan to start chemotherapy. In those moments, I had unsettling thoughts that not everyone was as healthy as they looked, or at least, that's what I suspected.

As I left the room, I glanced around, hoping to find the woman who had kindly offered me water earlier. But she had disappeared into the crowd, and I felt a pang of regret for not thanking her. Once more, we were wandering through another maze-like hallway. We entered an office that seemed to go on forever. A nurse by the door was calling out patients' names. In the midst of the crowd, there was an underlying unease, with voices sounding anxious. She called out the names, her loud voice perhaps providing a small bit of reassurance in this confusing situation.

After what felt like an endless forty-five minutes, I finally heard it – "Rachel! Rachel Ray!" Kenneth raises his hand, and we go inside. Stepping into the room, I'm hit by the feeling that I'm about to defend a thesis; there's a group of doctors, and the director is at the front. She starts by looking us up and down.

"Ah, a good-looking young couple! Your husband has a familiar look, like a movie star," she smiles. It's like we've stumbled into a fashion show or some secret event.

"I know my husband's got his charms, tall and chiseled jawline and all," I try to make sense of the situation, forcing a smile.

"Oh," the director doctor adds, "and your beautiful long blonde hair is simply lovely." Her smile seems a bit sarcastic. "Given your youthful beauty, I'll have you see our best doctor, Dr. Nola. She'll take care of your case."

We put on a smile, thanked her, and left the office.

The nurse told me that my appointment with Dr. Nola was set for tomorrow. We could finally figure things out and talk to her.

As we left that place, chaotic and filled with lost souls, my heart sank. It was a place without much hope. Once in the car, I turned to Kenneth and said,

"You told me the biopsy was fine! I don't get why you won't just tell me the truth. I deserve to know, whether it's good or bad. Can't you see that?" I spoke with frustration, raising my voice.

His eyes stayed so cold, no reaction at all. He was good at hiding his feelings, but I knew him well. There was something off, something not right.

"Everything's fine, but for extra safety, you'll get chemotherapy. Don't worry," he replied fast, but he didn't sound very reassuring. I felt like he was hiding something. The atmosphere was tense.

We took a drive through the busy streets of Tirane. We began in the city center, went by the pyramid, and finally reached the Block where I used to work. I could tell Kenneth was talking like this to stop me from asking more questions. So, I decided to keep my thoughts inside and tried my best to believe what he was saying.

I waved goodbye to Kenneth and climbed a few steps to reach my workplace on the first floor. I greeted the receptionist and spotted Jonna waiting on the second floor. She was a beacon of concern, exuding empathy that only a true friend could radiate. I could tell she was genuinely worried about me, perched on the edge of her seat, ready to offer comfort and support.

"Rachel, spill the beans! How did your doctor's appointment go? Did you finally finish that radiation therapy? What did the doctor say?" She asked with a mix of curiosity and concern.

I hesitated, struggling to put my roller coaster of emotions into words. "I have to go through another four months of chemotherapy," I finally admitted, my voice quivering.

"Wait a minute! You told me the biopsy was fine. Something doesn't make sense here. Why would they give you chemo if everything's okay?" she questioned, her determination unwavering.

"I don't know," I admitted. "I've asked Kenneth about it over and over, but he keeps saying everything's fine. But deep down, I can tell he's hiding something. I have the right to know what's really happening with my own body."

With a determined look in her eyes, she encouraged me, "You need to push harder, Rachel. Make him tell the truth because even if he's only sharing half of it, it won't help you. I'm here for whatever you need, as much as I can do. What's most important is that you recover and thrive." The suspense hung in the air, and I wondered what Kenneth was keeping from me.

As I walked into my office, I felt the immense weariness that weeks of radiation therapy had brought upon me. I was utterly exhausted. I informed my colleagues on the recruitment team that I would likely start chemotherapy in a month or two, pending a doctor's guidance tomorrow.

I remembered those days when, due to the exhaustion from radiation, I would sometimes doze off at my desk. We had a one-hour break, and I'd only take a brief ten-minute lunch break before locking the office door from the inside. I'd set an alarm on my phone to ensure I woke up on time. Even though I was still tired and would rest my head on the table for a while, those short rests helped me get through the day.

I was fortunate that there wasn't an overwhelming workload during that time. Nevertheless, I never neglected my responsibilities. I continued working and tried to maintain a semblance of normalcy. I was in charge of recruiting both Italian and English-speaking candidates, interviewing ten people at a time for each class. Later, I'd support them during their early days to boost their self-confidence at work.

I can say I felt good despite my exhaustion. I persevered, determined to stand tall and move forward. I always reminded myself, and still do, "Keep fighting until the end! Life is precious; do what you love and what fulfills you."

* * *

The next morning, we woke up early, eagerly awaiting our meeting with the doctor. In front of me, there was a woman who looked exhausted and could barely stand. So, I turned to Kenneth and said, "Let her go ahead, please, she can hardly stand."

"Sure," he replied. The woman gave us a grateful smile and thanked us. Albanians are naturally inquisitive, and they often can't resist asking questions, even if they might be painful. Another older woman glanced at me from top to bottom, seemingly concerned, and asked, "Who are you here for, dear? Are you here for someone else or for yourself?"

I was surprised by the audacity of her question. But then, I realized she was an older lady who might not have thought too much about her words. In a shaky voice, I replied, "I'm here for myself."

"That's so unfortunate at such a young age! I hope you get well soon," she said. I just said, "Thank you," and then it was our turn to go in.

"Hello! How are you?" Dr. Nola greeted us. She was so polite, educated, and professional. She knew how to make you feel at ease and optimistic. She stood tall and had a warm smile. "Rachel, you'll have only four chemotherapy sessions, once a month. They won't be as strong as some patients here. We'll start in two months to give you time to recover from the radiation. If you have any questions or concerns, please feel free to ask."

She was a friend of my husband's cousin, and we hoped that might make things easier. But as I looked around at all the people with no hair, I couldn't help but wonder the same thing.

"Doctor, will I lose my hair?"

That question bothered me a lot. I wondered if I would lose my hair and turn into a person that Kenneth wouldn't recognize. I felt more and more uneasy and anxious.

Ten

Chapter 10

I know many of you might be curious about what the doctor said in those important moments. I wish she hadn't said what she did. But here's what she told me:

"Rachel," she began, her voice calm and caring, "chemotherapy can be tough. You'll lose your hair, feel tired, get sick at times, lose weight, not feel like eating much, and might have some stomach problems. But please, don't worry about all this right now. We have some time to get ready. Focus on preparing for your first treatment. It's still September, and we're planning to start your therapy in November. Use this time to relax and take care of yourself. I'll give you some tests to do before the first session. I promise we'll make it as smooth as we can." She tried to give me hope with her words.

"Thank you," I said, my smile showing both gratitude and worry. The harsh reality of what was coming began to sink in.

As Kenneth drove me to work, I decided to follow Jonna's advice. I needed to confront the reality of our situation. Even though I had a sense of the truth, I wanted to hear it from him. Someone had to reveal what was really going on. I knew him well, and I knew how to get him to open up. This conversation would be tough for both of us, but it was necessary.

It was just the two of us in the car. He was driving, and I was in the passenger seat, buckling my seat belt. I took a deep breath and prepared to start the conversation in a way that would push him to talk.

"Now, you have to tell me what's going on, and tell me the truth! I'm not a child, and I can't handle any more lies. Don't you understand I need to know what's happening?" I raised my voice intentionally to provoke irritation.

"What are you talking about? Just sit there. What truth do you mean?" I could tell from his tone that he was getting irritated. That meant my approach was working. The conflict was growing stronger.

"Do you think I'm a kid? Do you think I haven't figured it out? Speak up, tell me what I already know. I'm not a fool who can't get it. I just want the truth," I ranted in the car, my anger boiling.

"Enough, I told you not to talk!" he snapped at me.

"Just tell me, for heaven's sake! I'm tired and sick of this! Tell me!" I shouted at him.

"Fine, you want the truth? Are you really ready to hear it? Okay! I'll tell you the truth. You're sick. The biopsy didn't go well; it's not okay.

Nothing is okay," Kenneth yelled at the top of his lungs, and it felt like an explosion had just gone off. The anger and tension in the situation were palpable.

He kept yelling and hitting the steering wheel. I could see he was really upset, hurt, and carrying a heavy burden. I knew he was trying not to hurt me or make me feel bad. I understood that! I knew he'd rather hurt himself than me. I knew it, and I knew it. But I had to know, and this was the only way he'd tell the truth. It was hard, but both of us needed to know what was coming. Only by knowing could we get ready for the battle with the right tools.

As Kenneth's words hung in the air, my emotions threatened to take over. Tears filled my eyes because the truth was so heavy. I turned my head and stared out the car window at the passing scenery. Everything outside looked blurry, just like the mess of feelings inside me.

With a shaky hand, I quickly wiped away the tears rolling down my cheeks, trying hard to hide my vulnerability from anyone around. A mix of emotions welled up in me, not just sadness, but a storm of feelings threatening to overwhelm.

I felt frustration deep in my chest, an exasperation with how unfairly life had treated us. There was bitterness too, bitter about the harsh challenge life had thrown our way.

Amid all these intense emotions, all I wanted was for him to talk to me, to share the weight of our truth. I hoped for him to trust me, just as I had always trusted him throughout our life together. That was the core of it all – a desperate plea for understanding, connection, and unity in the face of tough times. The emotions were running strong

I felt the weight of responsibility pushing me to go to work, knowing that our finances were strained and I couldn't afford to waste a single day. It's just not my style. However, on this particular day, I found myself torn, unsure if I could bring myself to go anywhere, except maybe not back home. All I yearned for was a place where I could be alone, hidden from prying eyes and the cacophony of the world. My emotions swirled within me, threatening to overwhelm my composure. I longed to unleash a scream that could vent my frustrations to the heavens, but I clenched my lips and remained in silence. That's where I found myself—right outside my workplace.

The anger inside me finally burst forth, and I vented it by forcefully slamming the car door shut. Kenneth's words were sharp and stung like daggers. "I understand your frustration, but I had no choice," I muttered, trying to rationalize my actions.

With determined steps, I ascended the stairs, masking my inner turmoil with a strained smile, until I reached the second floor. There, Jonna was waiting for my arrival. Without hesitation, I confessed to her, my voice trembling with the intensity of the moment.

"You were right," I began, "He wasn't honest. Chemotherapy is looming, and the biopsy delivered grim news. I have some time to prepare; my first therapy session is scheduled for November."

The dramatic intensity of that moment weighed heavily upon me.

Jonna responded gently, "Ray, we all deserve the truth, whether it brings joy or sorrow. Lying to someone, even if you believe it's for their own good, only leads to the opposite. You're intelligent and radiate positivity. Everything will work out," she assured me, lightly touching my shoulder.

With those comforting words, I entered my office, carrying a mixture of emotions and newfound answers.

** * **

Time felt like it was speeding up, flying by like a bird in the sky. Our family was sticking together, closer than ever. We spent weekends with my parents or went for coffee and walks. Everything seemed different now, more precious than ever. Even though we were sad and hurting, giving up wasn't an option for us.

Work had its own rhythm, and my colleagues felt like family. Some moments were beautiful but tiring. I started going to church more often, feeling closer to God and my faith. I felt a mix of fear and relief, knowing what was coming. I was relieved to prepare for another challenge, even though I didn't know how it would affect me. Would it be like crashing against a wall, or falling into an abyss where no one could reach me?

At first, we thought our son would be home during the first round of therapy, and later, both of us would go to stay with my parents in Gramsh. But I felt that a tough time was coming, and I wasn't sure how things would turn out. I knew we'd both need care, but I couldn't stand being in bed all day without doing anything.

So, when I talked to my aunt, she said that if I wanted something, I should just ask for it. I knew I would stay in Gramsh for a while, but staying inside all day wasn't my style. I thought I'd have some extra time, and maybe I could work on getting my driver's license. I know it might sound strange to think about getting a driver's license while going through four months of therapy, but that's just me. I like to keep myself busy to stop my mind from wandering.

* * *

On a lovely, sunny day, I sat with my colleagues, Greta, Kim, and Sido, in our cozy workplace courtyard. We sipped our coffee and enjoyed the warm sun. Our conversation flowed naturally as we chatted.

We started talking about my upcoming haircut, which was prompted by my upcoming chemotherapy. I joined in, holding my coffee cup, and said, "You know, folks, I think it's time for a haircut. My hair has gotten pretty wild."

Sido grinned and said, "Rachel, I've got the perfect hairstylist for you! He's like a hair wizard, and the best part is, he's nearby. You should give him a try."

Kim raised an eyebrow and asked, "Really? You're so confident in this mysterious 'hair magician.'"

Greta, curious as well, added, "Yeah, Sido, you're really talking this guy up. Is he as good as you say?"

Sido was full of excitement, nodding enthusiastically, and said, "Absolutely! He's like a hair magician, I promise. You won't be disappointed."

I chuckled and agreed, "Alright, Sido, you've convinced me. A little hair magic sounds fun. What's this guy's name?"

Sido, with a mischievous look, teased, "His name is Edward Scissorhands."

Laughter burst out among us, and even the people passing by couldn't help but join in. It was a moment of pure joy that turned our everyday chat into a memorable one.

Kim, between laughs, said, "Well, if Edward Scissorhands is in town, I'm in for a trim too!"

Greta, still giggling, added, "I'm up for it too. Getting a haircut from a legendary hair magician sounds like a blast."

Sido, playfully, wrapped it up, "Great! It's a plan, then. We're going on a group adventure tomorrow to meet Edward Scissorhands!"

* * *

The next day came, and we found ourselves, a bunch of friends with smiles and a pinch of curiosity, outside the charming and slightly odd hair salon. The outside was decorated with old-style posters and a mix of colorful chairs that hinted at the unique experience we were about to have.

As we entered the salon, a cheerful bell announced our arrival. Inside, creativity burst from every corner, with mirrors showing off various haircuts and styles. The air was filled with the scent of hair products and the gentle buzz of clippers, all while other clients chatted and laughed.

Edward Scissorhands, the stylist himself, looked like a character from a movie. His hair was a wild mix of colors, and he wore an outfit that was far from ordinary. He welcomed us with open arms and his scissors ready to work their magic.

Sido, known for her fearless nature, took the first chair with a playful wink. Edward's scissors moved with precision, creating a look that made Sido smile from ear to ear.

Kim couldn't resist making a joke as she got ready for her turn. "Hey, Edward, can you make me look like a rock star? Or maybe a disco queen from the '70s?"

Edward chuckled, his scissors dancing, "Darling, I'll make you shine brighter than a disco ball!"

Greta, always the optimist, chimed in from her chair, "Edward, I want a haircut that reflects my sunny personality. Can you do that?"

Edward replied with a twinkle in his eye, "Absolutely! I'll make sure your hair radiates sunshine!"

And when it was my turn, I couldn't resist teasing, "Edward, can you give me a haircut that hides my tears but still looks fabulous?"

Edward winked, "Darling, I'll give you a cut that turns those tears into sparkling gems."

As Edward continued to work his scissors, our laughter filled the salon. His unique style and incredible skill turned our haircuts into exciting journeys.

Upon leaving the salon, we were infused with newfound confidence. Our hair wasn't just different; it symbolized a fresh start. It also underscored the strength of our friendship and the power of humor during challenging times.

Edward Scissorhands hadn't merely transformed our hair; he had brought us closer as friends. For that, we were sincerely grateful. Little did we know, our adventures were just beginning. Me... I was preparing myself for the darkness that still feared might arrive sooner than expected.

Eleven

Chapter 11

As we hurried to the hospital, I felt a rush of fear and confusion. The city lights zipped by, matching the turmoil inside me. Kenneth's voice broke through the tension.

"Rachel, try to stay calm. We'll make sure you get the help you need," he assured me, his hands tight on the steering wheel.

Tears filled my eyes, and I nodded, gasping for air. The pain in my chest seemed unending, like something crushing me. We had to reach the hospital quickly.

Finally, we got to the hospital, but there was a big problem. The oncology department where I got chemo didn't have the right stuff for this emergency. So, we had to go to the regular emergency room. But there was an issue – we couldn't tell them I was getting chemo because they might say no, to treating me.

I told Kenneth quietly, "We can't let them know about the chemo. They might send us away."

He agreed, and we decided to keep my chemo a secret. It was risky, but we didn't want any delays. Time was super important, and we were determined to get the help I really needed.

We walked into the emergency room, which was full of doctors and nurses helping patients. The doctor there checked me quickly and hooked me up to some machines. These machines showed that I had tachycardia and a fast heartbeat.

The doctor said with urgency, "We need to act quickly. Give her medicine to calm her heart and nerves."

A nurse then gave me medicine that made my heart slow down and made me feel less scared. It was like a soothing relief, and I hoped the worst was over.

When I felt better, we went back home. In the car, Kenneth said, "Tomorrow, we'll call my cousin. He's a doctor and a close friend of your oncologist. He'll help us understand what's happening and why."

When we arrived home, I expressed our gratitude to his aunt for her support. Later, Kenneth drove her back to ensure her safe return.

The next day, Kenneth called Florence, "Hi Florence, how's it going?"

"Can I talk to you about something, cousin?" he asked, his tone filled with concern. "Yesterday, we were at the hospital with Rachel, and she had tachycardia that didn't improve. Is that something to be concerned about?"

With genuine concern, the cousin replied, "Well, the tachycardia is likely a side effect of the medications and treatments she's undergoing. I'll prescribe some sedatives to help her sleep and stay calm. She can take either half a pill or a whole one."

"Thank you! We'll chat later. I know you're at work," Kenneth expressed his gratitude.

Kenneth headed to work after dropping our son at daycare, leaving behind the morning hustle and bustle. Finally, I had a brief moment to myself, a cherished solitude within our home. After tidying things up, I decided it was time to enjoy a comforting shower.

My bathroom, a serene sanctuary, felt spacious and elegant with its sleek black tiles that subtly reflected glimpses of myself as I stood under the showerhead. While massaging shampoo into my hair, a sudden rush of fear overcame me. The fear I had been expecting and dreading was starting to come true.

In my hands, I held fragile strands of my hair, breaking free and drifting away, like leaves carried by the autumn wind. I had been noticing these signs every morning, more hair on my pillow, a painful reminder of the battle my body was facing. But deep down, I had hoped this decline would happen more slowly. As I watched my hair quiver in my trembling hands, my eyes filled with tears.

In those fragile moments, I let myself give in to my weakness, allowing my tears to flow freely, each drop a sign of the heavy, unspoken pain

I carried. I yearned for someone to comfort me, a person to talk to, but I was surrounded by solitude. It was a deep loneliness that felt impossible to break through, a feeling of being alone where my sorrow seemed to bounce back, unheard and misunderstood.

These were moments of intense pain, etched into my memory with a force that's hard to put into words. When I felt weak and exposed, I grappled with many uncertainties. I wondered how my relationship with Kenneth might change as I became this vulnerable version of myself. Would he still hold me close with the same love and care? Or would the sight of my altered appearance terrify him and create a divide in our once unbreakable bond?

And what about Liam, our beloved son? Would he, too, be scared or repulsed by his mother, who now looked so different? I couldn't help but imagine his innocent eyes widening at the sight of me without my usual hair, and I wondered how he'd perceive this change.

In the soothing embrace of the shower, as the water gradually turned colder, I found comfort in my solitary moment. I wished, if only for a little while, that I could stay there forever and let myself dissolve into the water, shedding the heavy weight of life. However, the cold water's bite on my skin acted as a gentle wake-up call, urging me to step out and face the reality beyond the shower's walls.

Terrified of confronting the extent of my hair loss, I carefully covered my head with a large, black hood. It was a shield, a disguise to hide my changing appearance from the world. It wasn't just about hiding from others but also from my own reflection in the mirror. Every morning, I feared looking at myself and fully accepting the changes my body was going through.

That afternoon, under the warm, golden sunlight, I went to pick up Liam from daycare. The playground resounded with the joyous laughter of children, a poignant reminder of the innocence and purity of youth. Among those children, he stood there with his tousled hair and bright, curious eyes, radiating an aura of innocence.

As I approached him, a hidden smile graced my lips beneath my hood. Liam's small, delicate fingers reached out, their curiosity piqued by the fabric concealing my head. He liked the texture and the mystery of the hood. His innocent interest brought a momentary lightness to my heavy heart.

On our way back home, Liam asked to be carried in my arms. My weakened body struggled to support him, and I did my best to hide the strain and fatigue that was wearing me down.

The short distance between the daycare center and our house seemed endless. The weight of my reality pressed down on me, making each step a challenge. I didn't just need a moment at the door; I needed time to gather the last shreds of my strength.

My neighbors couldn't help but notice the changes in me during this difficult time. Their expressions conveyed a mix of concern and curiosity. They seemed torn between offering help or asking how I was. Yet, fear or maybe a sense of intrusion kept them silent, creating a noticeable gap between us.

Fearing judgment and wanting to avoid those pitying looks or questions, I hid in our home. I closed the windows and blinds, trying to protect not only myself but also Liam from the unspoken truths that were changing our lives.

I eagerly awaited Kenneth's return from work. I wanted him to experience the joy of seeing our son play. But the guilt was heavy on my shoulders. I knew that by not being able to carry or play with Liam, I was taking away a simple joy from his childhood. Each moment I couldn't hold him felt like a piece of my motherhood slipping away.

We had to make a heart-wrenching decision. We needed help and support, and it was clear that Gramsh was the place to find it. My parents' love and assistance would provide the safety net we desperately needed. I couldn't bear the thought of leaving Liam alone during my hospital visits or when fatigue overwhelmed me.

One evening, I confessed to Kenneth through tears, "The pain of that reality haunted me every moment. But my love for our son pushed me to seek the best care and the strongest support, even if it meant being far away from him."

He looked at me, his eyes filled with the struggle and love we both carried. "It's a hard choice, but it's the right one for Liam and you," he comforted, reaching for my hand. "We'll get through this together. Liam will understand when he's older."

"I had a talk with Liam one evening, and I can still picture it clearly," I went on, the memory vivid in my mind. "I said, 'Liam, my sweet boy,' my voice shaking with emotion. 'We're going to stay with Grandma and Grandpa for a little while.'"

He tilted his head, showing his confusion, and asked, "Why, Mommy?" It broke my heart to hear him ask, but I kept my voice soft and said, "Mommy needs some extra help to get better. Grandma and Grandpa will take great care of both of us."

Having that talk with Liam was so hard, and the thought of not being with Kenneth, even if it's just for a while, was tough to handle. I knew we had to do it for Liam and me to get better. That night, my tears just wouldn't stop. I felt so sad, so lonely, and yet so full of love for Kenneth, understanding that this separation was something we couldn't avoid, even though it hurt so much.

But what comes next? What's in store for us? Will there still be an "us" when all of this is over? This was my biggest fear and one of the crossroads on where to step next...

Twelve

Chapter 12

Here we were in the small town of Gramsh: Liam, Kenneth, and me, in the cozy comfort of my childhood home. Every time we entered the house, it felt like stepping into a warm, safe place filled with love and unwavering support. My parents, Lina and Peter, had created a special home that made the world outside seem less scary. Their house was like a cozy symphony, and the air was filled with memories that embraced me like a loving hug.

My mother, Lina, was like a ray of sunshine that brightened every corner of the house. Even in her fifties, she had a timeless grace, and her smiling face always made me feel better when I had worries. She had a comforting roundness about her, a sign of her nurturing spirit that made everyone feel comfortable. As soon as you walked in the door, her lovely scent, a mixture of love and motherly care, would wrap around you. It's a smell that you remember like a favorite song. I really missed those moments, her scent, and her warm hugs. People say a mother's love is special, and Lina showed that in every way.

And then there was Peter, my dad, a strong and joyful presence in our lives. He had his special way of supporting us, often by having fun with Liam. Their moments of connection were a delight to watch, filled with laughter and happiness that filled the whole room. When Liam's eyes lit up in response to Peter's jokes and games, it showed how much a grandfather's love can be magical. It wasn't just play; it was a way of expressing love without words.

Peter's laughter was like the background music in our home, a tune that accompanied our lives through good times and tough times.

"Grandpa, can you tell me the story of the old oak tree again?" Liam would ask with excitement in his eyes.

"Oh, the old oak tree," Peter would respond, getting ready to tell a story, a mischievous twinkle in his eye. "Once upon a time, in a distant forest, there was a very old oak tree…"

Their laughter would fill the room, a perfect mix of youthful energy and wise experience. The walls of our home held onto these sounds, keeping them like a precious tapestry of shared moments.

Amidst all the happy moments and stories we shared, Gramsh felt like the most important place in the world. It was a spot where time seemed to slow down, giving us the chance to really enjoy every special moment.

Kenneth had come to stay with us for the weekend, but he had to go back to work on Monday. I was getting ready to start my driving lessons in a week. However, during those two days, I couldn't enjoy my usual cup of coffee. It tasted bitter and left a bad taste in my mouth.

The only things I could eat were a little bread and olives; everything else just didn't taste good. So, I made a choice to stop drinking coffee. I thought it was too acidic and believed it might help cleanse my body.

During those days and nights, we had a fire going and tried to relax by its warmth. But I was really low on energy, and I found it hard to do much. Because of the chemotherapy I was feeling more tired, felt weak, and could barely support my own body. Even simple things like going to the bathroom felt like a big task at times. Having Kenneth with me for those two days was a real blessing. His presence helped take my mind off the sadness I felt and the emotional walls were starting to build around me.

On Monday morning, my son woke up before me. He was like an early bird in our house, full of energy and excitement. This morning was no different. I could feel his little presence, lively and moving around. My father, seeing how enthusiastic Liam was, tried to guide him quietly and encourage him to let me sleep a bit longer. Their quiet voices and soft steps reassured me that they were taking care of everything, looking after Liam's needs and getting ready for the day.

But my own energy was at an all-time low, and I felt trapped by tiredness. Getting out of bed felt like a huge challenge. Even as the clock passed eleven in the morning, my body just wouldn't cooperate.

From the kitchen, I could hear the sounds of laughter, a sharp contrast to my own struggle. I tried with all my might to force myself to get up, to break free from the grip of exhaustion. I silently told myself to wake up, but it felt like I was in a vast, empty space, and my words echoed off the walls, unheard and fading into nothing.

In the middle of this tough fight, a touch of love and warmth broke through the darkness. My dad's hand gently rested on my shoulder, like a lifeline, pulling me back from the edge. His voice, filled with worry and affection, cut through the sadness, telling me to face the day.

"Rachel, wake up. Liam is missing you," he whispered, reminding me of my responsibilities and asking for company. "Come on! Try to wake up."

Those words carried a heavy meaning that lit a spark of determination in me. Liam needed his mom, and I couldn't let my own weakness keep me down. I gathered every bit of bravery and strength I had, fighting against the tiredness, and slowly getting out of bed. For Liam, and for my family, I was determined to win this battle inside me.

Summoning all my energy, I managed to make my way to the kitchen. Each step felt like a long and difficult journey like I was running a marathon against my own body. When I entered the kitchen, I was greeted by the smell of breakfast, a comforting scent that briefly lifted my spirits.

Liam, still full of morning energy, rushed over to me with a big smile. "Mommy, you're awake!" he said, his eyes shining with happiness.

I managed to give a small smile and gently touched his cheek. "Of course, my dear. How could I stay in bed when I get to see you?"

My mom, Lina, looked at me with worry. "You should eat, dear. It will give you some strength," she encouraged, her love and concern clear in her eyes.

"I'll do my best," I whispered, knowing I had to try.

Dad, always there to support me, added, "Take it slow, Rachel. We're here for you."

Sitting at the table, I took a small bite of toast, and it felt like an achievement. My family's support and love wrapped around me like a warm, comforting blanket, giving me the strength to keep going. Liam, sitting nearby, talked excitedly about his adventures, filling the room with his youthful energy and reminding me of the beauty still present in the world.

"Mommy, I drew a picture for you today," Liam said with excitement, waving a piece of paper in the air.

Lina gently took the drawing and looked at it in wonder. "Oh, it's beautiful, sweetheart! You're quite the artist."

I managed to put on a real smile, feeling proud of my son's creativity. "You're amazing, Liam. Can you tell me about your drawing?"

Liam excitedly started explaining his masterpiece and his enthusiasm was infectious. The room seemed a bit brighter, a little warmer, as his pure joy filled the air.

Throughout the day, I tried my best to save my energy. I watched as Liam played with clothes, tossing them around and having fun. Eventually, I gave him an empty suitcase, and he happily climbed inside, giggling as if he'd found a new treasure. Even though I was very low on energy and couldn't actively join in his play, I sat there, captivated by his innocence and happiness, trying to cherish every precious moment.

As the day turned into night, my tiredness became more noticeable.

Despite my own struggles with illness, I made sure to be there for Liam at bedtime. Holding him close, I breathed in his scent—his smell was like a comforting tune that eased my worried soul. The rhythm of his breath against my chest was like a soothing lullaby that took me to a peaceful place amidst the storm of my health problems.

However, my struggle wasn't finished. Every night, I took pills to slow down my fast-beating heart, a small but crucial routine to deal with the constant tachycardia that troubled me. These pills were like a lifeline, giving me a bit of steadiness in the midst of my inner turmoil. They served as a reminder of how fragile I was and how much strength it required to get through each day.

* * *

I completely forgot about my incredible sister, Flora. How could I do that? She's been by my side in both the best and toughest moments. Flora and I have always been close, sharing conversations, and tea, and supporting each other through everything. To me, she's not just a cousin; she's like a big sister, even though she's younger but taller than me. That's why I call her my big sister. She's the best—so mature and sometimes a little stubborn. Flora is a bit reserved; she doesn't reveal everything about herself. But her support, her presence, and everything she does, she's always there. She's a beautiful girl with a tall figure, long brown hair, and expressive eyes. She's usually straightforward when she talks but also fair and to the point.

One evening, Flora and I were sitting in our cozy living room, enjoying our favorite tea. Flora grinned mischievously and said, "Remember the time we tried to bake that cake, and it turned into a brick?"

I chuckled, thinking back to that disaster. "Oh, how could I forget? We followed the recipe step by step, and it still ended up looking like a construction material!"

Flora had a hearty laugh, saying, "Well, we made a great team, at least in making bricks, if not so much in making cakes."

And then, we were off on a trip down memory lane, sharing jokes and stories that only we could understand. Flora had a way of making even the simplest moments hilarious. Our laughter filled the room, echoing the bond that went beyond being cousins—truly, she was my big sister in every sense.

"Hey, remember the time you tried to teach me to dance, and we ended up in a tangle of limbs?" Flora teased, her eyes sparkling with mirth.

"How could I forget? I'm surprised we didn't trip over ourselves more often," I replied, laughter bubbling up once again.

"Oh wait wait wait I almost forgot about this other story. It is beyond great!", Flora recalled.

"Do you remember that one night when my mom checked on us in the middle of the night, and we got really scared?" she said, a playful smile on her face.

I couldn't help but grin, "Oh, that night! How could I ever forget?"

It was a night from our childhood, a night of innocent fears and surprises we didn't see coming. It was the night when Aunt Donna, Flora's mom, played some strange and spooky tricks on us. The room was filled with the comforting smell of vanilla, a scent that still lingers in my memories.

"The lights were off," she continued, "and my mom, wearing her long white nightgown, held a flickering candle, making the room look eerie yet cozy."

I added, "We were wide-eyed, and then she quietly entered our room, checking on us. It felt like a scene from a ghost story!"

For a moment, fear got the best of us as our imaginations ran wild, but then the fear lifted, and we burst into laughter, filling the room with our joyful giggles. The memories of that night became a part of our hearts, a mix of childhood fright and the happiness of shared laughter.

"And then," I chimed in, still chuckling at the memory, "we realized it was Aunt Donna, and we laughed until our stomachs hurt."

Flora nodded, saying, "My mom was really good at turning even the scariest moments into laughter. She's amazing."

In that cozy room, with a soft lamp's gentle glow and the lingering smell of tea, we found comfort in each other's company. We valued the beautiful collection of memories that shaped our lives, like a colorful mosaic. Aunt Donna's playful tricks were just one vibrant piece in that mosaic, always making us smile and reminding us of the magic in our shared past.

After we had a good laugh, we tried to go to sleep...

But then something happened that I had seen coming in my dreams.

It was like the universe was unfolding a story we had glimpsed in our own thoughts. The room, which had been filled with laughter and warmth, suddenly felt colder. Shadows played eerie games, making it seem like they were sharing secrets. The happy memories of Aunt Donna's stories now seemed a bit unsettling, and we both felt uneasy as if we were anticipating something we couldn't quite grasp.

Flora asked in a soft, hesitant voice, "What did you dream?"

I hesitated, trying to find the right words to explain the dream that had been haunting my nights. "It's… hard to put into words. It felt like déjà vu but in a dream. The same place, the same feeling that something big was about to happen."

The candle's flame wavered, stretching shadows across the room, transforming it into an eerie place where the line between reality and dreams blurred. We sat in silence, each of us lost in our own thoughts, trying to make sense of the puzzling messages that dreams often carried.

As the night continued, the air became heavy with tension, our minds racing to understand the dream's meaning. It felt like we were standing on the edge of an unknown abyss, not sure what lay ahead, but unable to resist the pull of destiny.

I could only wait, certain that the answers would arrive, revealing the hidden secrets of my dreams. The candle's flickering flame mirrored my inner uncertainty, and I readied myself for whatever lay ahead. I was prepared to face the mystery that had transitioned from the dream realm into my reality.

Thirteen

Chapter 13

I never could find what that dream truly meant; it remained an enigma, haunting my thoughts like a persistent shadow. All I could recall was its continuation—an eerie dance between reality and the unknown.

One evening, the atmosphere grew heavy with an unsettling stillness. The wind outside whispered secrets of the night, and the moon hid behind a shroud of clouds, leaving the room dimly lit by the flickering candle's glow. Flora and I exchanged nervous glances, the premonition of that dream rekindling our fears.

"Do you remember the shadow man?" Flora whispered, her voice barely audible over the rustling leaves outside. "This… this feels worse than that."

Chills ran down my spine as I nodded, recalling the entity from my childhood nightmares—the shadow man that lurked in the corners of my mind. But this, this was an entity far more malevolent, its presence suffocating like a sinister fog.

That night, I fell into a troubled sleep. In my dream, I was lying on a bed, surrounded by heavy darkness. Above me, a gigantic, fiery creature hung there, glowing a hellish red, like it was burning. This mean thing wanted me, and its anger was so strong, it felt like it was choking the life out of me.

I felt desperate as the creature got closer, its fiery arms reaching for me as if it wanted to crush the last bit of courage left. I tried to fight back, but my feeble efforts were no match for its overpowering strength. My breaths became shallower, and my hold on consciousness slipped away.

I woke up suddenly, gasping for air, but the suffocating feeling stayed with me like it was crawling under my skin. My mom, hearing my cries, rushed into the room. She looked worried and asked, "What happened, dear? Are you okay?"

Trying to calm her concern, I stuttered, "It's nothing, sorry. Just a bad dream."

But it was more than just a dream; it was a glimpse into a nightmarish realm that had breached the boundaries of the mind. Fear had seeped into my reality, and I realized that the dream was a warning—a prelude to something much darker that awaited.

* * *

I knew my second therapy session was coming up, but before that, I wanted to get away from this small town. It's filled with memories, some wonderful, some really painful. Every part of this place has a story, with whispers from the past.

One day, as the sun made the cobbled streets glow with a golden light, I walked through the town center with my mom and Liam. We ended up in a charming square with a fountain. The sound of flowing water filled the air, making the city noise seem distant.

As I stood there, memories of my first love came rushing back, and I was overwhelmed. It was right here that I had my first kiss with him—a sweet and innocent moment that now felt like a lifetime ago. Tears filled my eyes, and emotions I didn't expect were welling up in me, ready to burst from my heart.

My mom saw me lost in thought and asked gently, "Are you okay, dear? Is everything alright?

I nodded and spoke softly, "Yes, Mom. Just memories, both lovely and sad."

Liam, sensing the serious mood, held my hand and said, "Mom, look at the water! It's dancing!"

His innocence brought a little happiness—a reminder that even when things are a bit sad, there's still hope and joy. I took a deep breath and pulled myself together, embracing the mix of sweet and bitter memories.

I needed a change of scenery, so I planned a trip to Tirana to see Kenneth. My heart longed to be with him and find comfort in our love.

On that day, I had to take the bus to Tirana since I didn't have a car, and Kenneth was the one with a car. When I got on the bus, I greeted the bus driver, and he kindly told me to sit in the two-seater section right behind him.

Before the bus started, I looked around and, to my surprise, saw an old friend coming my way. He had once wanted a romantic relationship with me, but now, fate had us meet again. I felt a bit panicked, trying to hide my condition and sickness. I slowly pulled the hood of my winter coat over my head, hoping he wouldn't recognize me.

"Oh no, he's getting too close, too close…" I whispered to myself as he sat down in the seat next to me. I couldn't help but think about my past beauty and how it contrasted with my current reality. "I used to be one of the prettiest girls in town. Look at me now. I'm so pitiful. You probably can't even stand to look at me," I thought, feeling a deep sense of despair.

He broke the silence by saying hello and asking about Kenneth. I hesitated for a moment, thinking about how to respond, and finally said, "I'm good, and you?"

We had a tense but seemingly normal conversation. I couldn't believe he didn't mention anything about my illness. Gramsh was a small town where it seemed like everyone knew everything about everyone, so his silence on the matter was unexpected.

I knew that when I got to Tirana, Kenneth would be there, waiting for me. When the bus came to a stop, he turned to me and asked, "Do you need help with anything?"

"No, thank you. I don't have much with me, just myself," I said, a little smile on my face. I greeted him and made my way toward the exit.

Kenneth was waiting for me near the bus stop, where he had parked his car, making it easy to switch from the bus to the car. I had missed his comforting eyes and his constant support.

After a week of not seeing each other, we finally sat down for a meal together. It was nice to have Kenneth there, and we picked a cozy restaurant in Tirana for our reunion. The place had a warm atmosphere, perfect for catching up and finding comfort in each other's company.

"So, what's new?" Kenneth asked, taking a sip of his drink.

"I'm managing, taking it one day at a time," I replied, trying to keep things light.

He nodded, "Yeah, I understand. It's been a busy week for me too."

I liked that Kenneth didn't dwell too much on emotions. He was always straightforward and practical.

"Weekends without you always feel so long," I said, a bit of longing in my voice.

"I know what you mean," he said, a real smile appearing. "It's great to be back with you."

We started talking about lighter stuff, letting go of the worries from the past week. In that moment, with shared laughter and delicious food, life almost felt normal, even if it was just for a while.

He sat there, looking calm, acting like everything was okay. To him, things were normal, and he missed me. I couldn't help but wonder silently, "How can you miss me? I feel like I'm nothing right now."

Watching him, I could tell he wanted to be close to me that night. It was clear in the way he looked at me and his gentle gestures. He was showing me that, for him, nothing had changed. But inside, I felt really tired, and I was uncomfortable with my own body.

Doubts filled my mind, and I wasn't sure if I was ready for what he wanted, for the closeness he seemed to need. The battle between my feelings for him and my exhaustion tore me apart, leaving me unable to decide. With every passing moment, my own limitations weighed heavy on my heart.

After dinner, we went home, both of us needing some rest. He opened the door, a door that used to welcome the laughter and talk of our family. Now, the house was eerily quiet. It was a silence that cut through me, stirring up anger and sadness. But I kept it all hidden behind a fake smile, a mask I had gotten really good at.

"I hate this silence so much," I said, my words showing the anger I felt, even though I was trying to smile and hide my inner turmoil.

We changed into comfy clothes, hoping to relax by watching a movie as bedtime got closer. He tried to tell jokes, attempting to make me smile. But I knew what he really wanted. It was clear tonight. He desired me, my body, and my affection. His passion burned strong, undeterred by our circumstances. I could feel the intensity of his desire, just like it was before as if nothing had changed.

"Is this real or is he pretending?" I wondered, struggling with mixed thoughts and emotions. I was torn between giving in to his desire and the fear of showing my vulnerability. The unspoken tension between us filled the room, adding complexity to our already complicated dance of emotions.

We lay in our bed, and at that moment, it felt strange and unfamiliar. He started to kiss me and touch my body. His kisses were just as passionate as before, showing he missed me. I missed him too. I was scared and emotional in those moments.

"How can you still want me, even when I'm at my worst? How?" These questions and insecurities only made me want him more.

But he was still there… He was not stopping himself from kissing in a soft and passionate way. Hugging even more, showing that he missed me. He missed me, not my body, just me… with the bad and the good things, just Rachel…

* * *

The next day, I had to go to the hospital for some tests to see how my body was doing before I could talk to my doctor about the results. After the tests, I planned to meet up with my cousin Julia because I wanted to buy a wig. I thought getting a wig would help me feel better about myself and make it less obvious that I was sick. I really didn't want people to know about my illness.

As we walked into the wig store, Julia said, "Let's find a wig that looks natural on you, something that suits you well."

I agreed and said, "I just want to feel like myself again."

We found a blonde wig that wasn't too expensive. After buying it, I asked Julia if she knew a good hairdresser who could add some highlights to make the wig look more real and cover my forehead.

"Do you know a good hairdresser nearby?" I asked Julia.

"Yeah, I do. Let's go there," Julia said, leading the way to the salon.

When we got inside, the hairdresser welcomed us with a friendly smile and asked, "Hello! How can I help you today?"

"I just got this wig," I told the hairdresser while showing it to her. "I want it to look more like my real hair."

The hairdresser smiled and said, "Sure, we can make it better by adding some highlights and styling it to match your style."

After the makeover, I put on the wig, and it looked amazing. To make it even more convincing, I wore a black cap that hid the fact that I was wearing a wig.

"I can't believe how natural it looks," I said to Julia, feeling really thankful.

Julia smiled and said, "You look fantastic! Let's add some makeup and get your nails done to finish the whole look."

"That sounds great," I said, starting to feel excited. "Thank you for being here with me, Julia."

As I looked at myself in the mirror, all done up with styled hair, and makeup, and wearing a beautiful outfit, I felt something hard to put into words. It was like, for a brief moment, I was transported back to my old life – a life I used to hate but now longed for so deeply. After having a cup of tea with Julia, we made our way to the hospital together, supporting each other along the way.

Even now, I can't forget how much Julia was there for me during those tough and dark days. When everything was uncertain, and people didn't know what to do or say, she was a constant presence, a glimmer of hope in the heavy darkness that filled the room.

As we walked down the hospital's dimly lit corridor, the flickering lights cast eerie shadows, making the already gloomy atmosphere reflect how I felt inside. The sterile smell of disinfectants and the distant, muffled sounds of medical equipment only added to the uneasiness of the moment.

"Rachel, your hair looks amazing. So natural – I can hardly tell it's not your own," the nurse exclaimed in amazement as we entered the hospital. Her words broke through the tension in the air.

"Thank you," I said softly, my voice filled with gratitude and humility. I lowered my head with a shy smile, trying to hide the tears welling up in my eyes.

The battle I was going through felt incredibly heavy, and even the smallest acts of kindness seemed like a lifeline in the middle of a stormy sea.

Once again, I found myself in that small bed surrounded by curtains.

The fancy decorations that once seemed unimportant now didn't matter compared to the fight going on inside me. The room was pretty dark, with only a faint light from the hallway making strange shapes on the walls, which matched the darkness I felt in my heart. This day was a bit quieter than the others, but the quietness made the emotional storm inside me seem even louder. Without realizing it, I had fallen asleep, with Julia right there, watching over me as the medicine dripped into my veins, ready to call the nurse for the next steps. Oddly, I felt even more tired this time, like I had small weights on my eyelids, each one representing my worries.

From a distance, I heard a soft voice telling me to wake up.

"Rachel, open your eyes. It's time to wake up," Julia gently shook me.

It took a lot of effort, but I managed to open my eyes and slowly move my arms and legs.

"I'm sorry, I must have dozed off."

It was already nighttime. I knew Kenneth would finish work early that evening, so he waited for us outside. Once we got into the car, we quickly dropped Julia off at her bus stop to make sure she got home safely. During the ride back, I couldn't say a word or even move a finger. I felt completely drained like I had lost control over my own body. It was a horrible feeling, making me feel weak and unable to do anything.

Finally, Kenneth broke the heavy silence, saying, "Is this how you feel after coming out of there?"

"What do you think?" I answered with a pause, finding it tough to speak.

The air was heavy. Kenneth embraced me and assisted me in getting out of the car and into the house. I changed into different clothes and lay down on the couch.

"Did you make dinner?" Kenneth asked.

"Yeah, it's in the oven. Just need to heat it up."

"Okay," he said.

I couldn't even stay on the couch, so I told him I needed to go to bed. I was incredibly tired, and I didn't feel like myself at all. It felt like a huge effort to get my body to our bedroom like it was really far away. I felt so awful that I can't even explain how it felt. It was just too much, and all I wanted was to use the bathroom and get some sleep. I was yearning for rest, to fall into a deep, deep sleep. I remember putting my head on the pillow, and then everything went blank… just blank…

Fourteen

Chapter 14

I woke up in my bed and blinked my eyes open. The ceiling above me was really dark, and the window bars were shut tight to block out the morning sun. Kenneth always did this because he knew I liked it dark and cool. It gave me a sense of comfort. I wasn't much of a fan of sunlight, but I loved the sound of rain and the chilly weather. When the rain fell, I could listen to it for hours, watching it make patterns on the window or the balcony while I wrote on my laptop. In those moments, it felt like I was in different places and situations that I could be, just with my vivid imagination. All my worries seemed to fade away, and I could explore my thoughts in a world that felt like it was made just for me.

I really didn't want to get out of bed that day. I just wanted to stay there, wrapped up in blankets all day long. But then, my dad called. I really didn't want to pick up the phone. I just wanted to stay warm and cozy in my bed. I didn't want to do anything, not even eat or drink. Actually, food has been a problem for me lately. But the phone kept ringing, and

I knew that if I didn't answer, my dad would get really worried. So, even though I felt so lazy, I reached for the small table where the phone was and answered with a weak and quiet voice.

"Morning, Dad!"

"Morning, Ray. Are you still in bed? Come on, sleepyhead. It's not good to sleep too much; it can make you feel slow and tired."

"Okay, I'm getting up slowly. I'm getting up," I said these words like I was trying to convince myself.

"Look, someone wants to talk to Mom. Come on, Liam, talk to Mom," Dad called.

"Mom, where are you? Why aren't you with me?" Liam's sweet voice came from the other side. It hurt to hear his questions, but I pushed down that bad feeling and the pain inside. I tried to sound happy and said, "Mom is at work right now, but I won't be too long. I'll come to you soon, my love." I tried to pretend I was smiling.

"Okay, Mom. But don't be too long. I went out with Grandpa for coffee, and I played with my toys," Liam told me on the other end of the phone.

"Ray, come on! Make something to eat or just order takeout," Dad told me.

"I'll get up, I promise. We'll talk later. Kenneth is calling," I said before hanging up.

"Hey there, how are you doing? Have you gotten out of bed yet? Are you about to explode?" he asked, clearly worried.

"I'm starting to get up now. Everyone is telling me I should, and it's driving me a bit crazy. I'm really tired, and I just want to stay in bed. Ugh!" I replied, and you could hear how tired I was in my voice.

"They're bringing you lunch. What would you like to order?" he asked.

"Just a salad and a bit of risotto, please. Thanks!" I said, trying to sound more cheerful.

"Great! It'll be there in thirty minutes, right on time. Oh, Neta suggested going to the movies today," Kenneth mentioned.

"I can't do it today. I'm not in the right frame of mind. I need some time to gather myself. Maybe we can plan for dinner tomorrow or the day after, please?" I asked.

"Okay, let's plan for the day after, then. Just don't stay in bed. Get up," he encouraged.

"Okay," I replied, but inside, I felt a little disheartened by what he said.

Today, everything just felt wrong. Sometimes, even when you act like you're okay and put on a brave face, deep down, you know it's not true. You tell yourself you're fine and strong, but the truth is, you're worn out. You can't keep going like this. All you want is to lie down in a dark room and shut out the world. You need someone to listen and understand. Pretending to be okay all the time, is too much. You want to scream and let out all the pain and frustration you've been holding inside. But it feels like no one can hear you or truly get what you're going through. You wish you had someone to lean on, someone to cry or yell with, but you feel so alone. These thoughts were always racing in my mind like a never-ending storm.

The delivery person brought my food, and I left a tip to thank them. But as soon as I got my meal, I quickly closed the door. I felt uneasy and didn't want anyone from the neighborhood to see me. I felt embarrassed about my situation and didn't want anyone to witness it. In the kitchen, I found a comfortable spot to sit. Although it was a big space, the kitchen felt unusually large. I moved from the corner table to the sofa and started to eat my meal, taking small bites because my stomach didn't feel quite right.

* * *

The days were passing by, and today was the day we had planned to go to the movies. To be honest, I didn't feel like it at all right now. But I couldn't say no. They were really trying to cheer me up and make me smile. Deep down, all I wanted was to sleep and relax. I was so tired and drained that my body was just following my thoughts, struggling to keep going.

When we got to the cinema, we got some popcorn and found our seats. Neta was a vibrant and lively person, and her smile could light up any room. She had this infectious energy and couldn't help but express herself. But this time, her fiance, Henry, spoke first.

"Neta, I heard this is one of the best movies. Are you excited?" Henry asked, trying to bring some excitement.

"Yeah, it's supposed to be really good. I'm looking forward to it," Neta replied, her eyes filled with anticipation.

I managed a smile, trying to match their enthusiasm. "Yeah, I've heard great things about it too. It should be fun."

As the movie started, I tried to immerse myself in the plot, to forget about my weariness. Neta and Henry seemed so engrossed, sharing occasional whispered comments about the scenes.

As the movie began, I tried to lose myself in the story, to forget how tired I was. Neta and Henry were so into it, whispering to each other from time to time about what was happening on the screen.

After a really intense part of the movie, Neta leaned over and said, "This is so exciting, isn't it? I love the suspense."

Henry added, "Absolutely! The way they filmed it is impressive."

I nodded, grateful that they were trying to include me in the conversation. Even though I was so tired, their company made the experience a little more bearable.

When the movie ended and the credits rolled, Neta had an idea. She said, "Let's capture this moment with a picture, all of us together."

Even though I didn't really want to, I managed a weak smile for the photo. When we looked at it later, you could see from my expression that I wasn't doing well these days.

* * *

During weekends, Kenneth and I had a special routine. We'd visit Gramsh, a place we both enjoyed. On Mondays, I had driving lessons with my instructor. I knew the basics, but there was still a lot to learn. Liam, our son, always had a bright smile when he saw us. My mom would cook my favorite dish, chicken and rice in a pot, which I still can't resist. I made sure to have some bone broth too, which was believed to help my body heal.

On weekends, my family and I would go to a coffee shop where Liam played with his toys and had a great time. It felt like a brief moment of normalcy. But some days, my anger and frustration would take over, and I'd snap at my mom, dad, or even Liam. Even though they didn't deserve it. It was like all my irritation and resentment were aimed at the situation I was in, a situation I didn't want to talk about. Even though my loved ones were there for me, it felt like no one really understood.

I took sedatives every morning and night to stay calm and sleep. Even though I was always tired, giving up wasn't an option. My seventh driving lesson was coming up next Monday. I had the basics down, but sometimes my mind wandered.

Gramsh, a small town, didn't have a bustling highway scene. The car we were using was a really old 270 Benx, a manual one, like something out of the Flintstones era. It was just me and the instructor, a serious guy with a thinning hairline. I'm pretty sure he was pushing sixty. He didn't chat much, a few words here and there was his way of teaching.

But then, out of the blue, an unexpected guest hopped into the car. My nerves decided to throw a wild party, and my hands were sweating like they were having a dance-off. Strangely, I started making all the wrong turns, and it felt like the car had a mind of its own. When the guy who hitched a ride with us got out, Mr. Instructor, as calm as a cucumber, said, "Rachel, what happened? You were doing great, and then suddenly, it got chaotic. You're scaring me."

I grinned and said, "Oops, my bad. I guess I got a little too excited about driving."

As we pulled back and aimed for a parking spot, I spotted Liam, my son, hanging out with his grandpa. I gave him a big hug, and he blurted out, "Mom, Mom! That guy took your car!"

I burst into laughter and said, "Ha-ha! No, kiddo, that's not Mom's car. That's the instructor's funky ride. Mom's just learning to drive it.

I sat on the couch, deep in thought, realizing it had been a whole week since some of Flora's cousins had last visited her house. One of her cousins used to catch my eye, but that feeling had faded with time. We've all grown older, and our views have shifted. I'm grateful for my loving family, and I cherish them every day. As the sun set and painted the sky with fiery colors, I took my usual walk to the driving course. That evening, the shadows danced around me, darkening the city streets. I wore a long, flowing black coat that concealed who I was in those days. A hood covered my face, and I had a blonde wig resting on my shoulders. My transformation wasn't complete until I applied makeup to hide any signs of vulnerability. With black eyeliner framing my eyes and lips painted with long-lasting lipstick, I wore a mysterious smile. No one could guess the turmoil I was concealing behind my mask.

Lost in my thoughts, I kept my head down, when suddenly, a car horn blared, startling me. I looked up and saw a car coming toward me, which was unexpected. Through the dim light, I recognized someone from my past. I used to know this person well and had strong feelings for him.

I heard an unfamiliar voice calling my name from a car, "Rachel! Rachel!" I felt a mix of surprise and fear, wondering who it could be. The only people I knew with a car were Kenneth and his brother Karter, but the voice and the car didn't belong to them. When I looked inside the car, I saw a smiling face that I thought I recognized…

Then, the back window rolled down, and I saw Flora in the car. I tried to stop myself and take another look. Yes, it was her.

"Rachel, Rachel! Hi! Stop for a second," Flora tried to get my attention.

Feeling unsure and insecure, I greeted them with, "Hi, guys! How are you? How have you been?"

Den, whom I hadn't seen in a long time, suddenly got out of the car. He walked over with a confident stride and a calm presence. Our eyes met, and he broke the silence.

"Rachel, how have you been? I love your new look. You don't have the typical Albanian vibe, more like a Russian or Polish beauty."

Trying to smile, I replied, "Thank you, Den. It's good to see you."

"Would you like to join us for dinner tonight?" Den asked.

I mumbled my response, "Um…"

"Come on, Rachel! Please, we'd really like you to come. I'm insisting," Ella, his sister, pressed on, joined by a chorus of voices.

"I'll try," I replied, my uncertainty making it hard to decide. I went to my driving lesson after saying hi to everyone. But I couldn't stop thinking about whether I should join them and see Deni again. He was someone I had a crush on when I was a teenager. I wondered why I should go, and I thought maybe they were just being kind. It didn't make much sense to me, and I couldn't make up my mind.

Fifteen

Chapter 15

I felt extremely bored as if time had become really slow. But the idea of meeting my cousin and friends for some drinks at the restaurant felt like a shining hope in the middle of this suffocating boredom. So, I quickly sent a message to Flora, who was my connection to a fun evening.

As I strolled down the dimly lit street, the winter's chill seemed to penetrate not just my body, but also my very soul. The frosty air nipped at my cheeks, and the brittle silence hung in the atmosphere, reminding me of the brevity and harshness of the day.

The moment I arrived at the restaurant, warmth washed over me. Grinning faces and contagious laughter filled the air as I joined my cousin and friends around a grand table. I took my place next to Flora, but my attention couldn't help but gravitate towards Deni, the center of my intrigue. It was as though a portal had opened to the past, transporting me back to my teenage years. Yet, amidst all the changes that had occurred, the most significant transformation had taken place within me.

I looked at the table, filled with lamb, goat, and beef dishes. In the past, I used to enjoy them a lot, but now, if you ask me, I feel unsure about eating them, except for a small piece of beef. I stared at the feast, and then Deni spoke up, saying, "I can't understand how someone can eat the flesh of an animal that once lived and had a soul."

My head hung low, and I found myself intensely scrutinizing the meat on my plate. Uncertainty loomed as I hesitated to bring that small piece to my lips. It was as though the meat on my plate had taken on a menacing aura, and I half-expected it to bite back at me. With a delicate touch, I gingerly pushed the plate away, and a contented smile crept across my face, a silent acknowledgment of my evolving sensibilities.

I inclined my head ever so slightly, captivated by the flickering flames within the wood-burning stove. The wood crackled and swayed in harmony with the music, casting dancing shadows across the cozy, wood-adorned room. Then, as if summoned by a spell, Greek music suddenly filled the air. In the intimate, timber-clad space, Ella and her husband embarked on a dance that was nothing short of enchanting. Their movements were like poetry in motion, an embodiment of profound love and tenderness. It was palpable in every graceful step, a testament to the deep connection they shared. Like any couple, they had undoubtedly faced their share of life's trials, yet their love and mutual respect were a rarity, a gem in the rough of human relationships. Witnessing their profound connection was a heartwarming experience.

By my side, Flora stood beaming alongside her fiance, their smiles echoing the warmth of the setting. But despite the beauty that enveloped me, a lingering sense of absence gnawed at my heart – a longing for my family and the life I once knew. My yearning for those moments of laughter and togetherness was almost unbearable.

Lost in my thoughts and fueled by the two glasses of red wine I had enjoyed, my phone rang, and it was Kenneth on the line. The din inside the restaurant made it difficult to hear, so I stepped outside for a more private conversation.

"Hey, Rachel, how's your evening going, sweetheart?" Kenneth's familiar voice greeted me, a nightly ritual.

"I'm good," I answered a little quickly. "We're with Flora, my aunt, Mike, Ella, her husband, and Deni. We're having dinner late, and we might go home soon." I decided to tell Kenneth everything at once because he sometimes got jealous for no reason. It felt smarter to prevent any confusion rather than let it turn into pointless arguments later.

"Alright, enjoy your evening. Tell me when you're back home," Kenneth said calmly.

"Sure thing, sweetheart. We'll talk later. Love you a lot," I replied.

"Love you more," he responded, as he always did.

The evening at the restaurant was filled with happiness and a cozy feeling. The air was full of laughter and lively conversations. Our food was not only tasty but also made better by the company of people who felt like family. The night was vibrant and full of life, which was quite different from the quiet moment I stepped out to have a sincere talk with Kenneth, as it was late, and he called me again.

Beneath the starry sky, a gentle breeze brushed against my skin, and soft music in the distance added to the enchanting mood. On the other end of the call, Kenneth's voice was like a steady anchor, giving me comfort and reassurance.

"Rachel, take your time, have fun, and be safe. Don't worry about me. I'll be here, waiting for you," he said. His words wrapped around me like a warm hug, making me feel calm and secure.

"Thank you, Kenneth. Your understanding means the world to me," I replied, overwhelmed with gratitude for the night's revelry but still yearning for the comforting embrace of home.

I went back to the restaurant and rejoined my friends. Knowing Kenneth was always there for me, the night stayed full of happiness and strong connections. We danced to the music, shared stories, and enjoyed our special talks, feeling our friendship get even stronger and more meaningful.

Deni, the embodiment of chivalry, graciously took on the role of our designated driver, ensuring that each of us arrived safely at our own doorstep. His presence exuded an aura of quiet strength and genuine care, his eyes radiating a warmth that seemed to reach the depths of my soul. Every glance and gesture spoke volumes of an affectionate and nurturing connection that had blossomed over the course of the evening.

As Deni deftly navigated the serene, dimly lit streets, it felt as though the car itself held its breath, cocooning us in an atmosphere charged with emotions left unsaid. My heart beat in sync with this unspoken connection that seemed to envelop us, with the majority of the emotions emanating from Deni's side, painting the journey with a tapestry of feelings that left an indelible mark on my heart.

Sensing the unspoken weight of Deni's emotions, I finally broke the silence. I turned to him with a soft smile, a veil that thinly concealed the curiosity and tenderness shimmering in my eyes. My voice, hushed to a mere whisper, carried my heartfelt gratitude, "Deni, I want to express my deepest thanks for being our guiding light tonight, for taking such good care of us."

Deni's gaze locked onto mine, his eyes glistening with a wellspring of emotions that transcended the need for words. His voice, deep and velvety, resonated through the car as he replied, "Rachel, it's been my absolute pleasure. I just wanted to make sure everyone had an unforgettable evening and returned home safely."

A gentle, knowing smile danced upon his lips, as though he harbored secrets of the heart that eluded verbal expression. In that fleeting moment, within the sanctum of the car, it felt as though our connection had deepened, our unspoken emotions pirouetting in the ethereal space between us. The air itself seemed charged with anticipation and the budding promise of romance, as the magnetic pull of our bond became increasingly impossible to ignore.

Yet, my lips could muster no more than a simple "Goodnight." I opened the car door and hastened on my way home. In that instant, the profound depth of my love for my family and the immense gratitude I held for every shared moment etched itself into my heart, an indelible mark of cherished emotions.

When I got back home, I walked in quietly, and in the soft light of the room, I saw my son sleeping peacefully. His calm face made my heart feel so full, reminding me that, at that moment, I didn't need anything else. It was a simple but precious sight that filled me with deep thankfulness for the richness of my life.

As the evening came to an end, we left the get-together, feeling tired but with our spirits lifted high. The happiness of spending time with friends and the sounds of their laughter still echoed in my heart. In the quiet of my bedroom, I had a happy smile on my face, showing how much I appreciated everything.

The night showed me how much love and help I had from the people around me. In these special moments, life revealed its true and simple beauty.

* * *

I'd been studying hard for my driving license test for over a week, and even though I knew they'd help with the theory part, that section always made me a bit nervous.

Someone had done me a favor, giving me this chance, and I felt both grateful and uncertain about what to expect. So, I worked diligently, getting myself ready for the challenge. One early morning, we set out for the test. It was just the three of us: me, my former driving instructor, and my ex-high school teacher whom I wasn't a fan of. He was a tall guy, really tall. He walked with such confidence that it felt like the ground trembled beneath him. He was super smart, but he often got lost in his thoughts, a bit absent-minded. In a way, he was scatterbrained, but he carried himself with the belief that the test was just a formality. Despite being introverted, he exuded a sense of assurance that was hard to miss.

When we arrived at the building didn't have to wait outside for long; it was time for the written test. One by one, we entered the room, had our pictures taken, and got ready for the challenge. As I went through the questions, a few of them puzzled me, and I wasn't sure if I got them right. Just when I was feeling uncertain, an unexpected helper came to my rescue, but let's not get into the details. Surprisingly, with their assistance, I managed to pass the test. However, my instructor didn't do as well, and he was disappointed he couldn't win for all of us.

On our way out, I led the group, and my old teacher followed, voicing his frustration to the instructor. "You know," he grumbled, "I've been driving for a long time, and this computer thinks it can beat me with its tricky questions!"

The instructor chuckled and nodded in understanding. "It can be quite tough, indeed. But don't worry; you'll do better next time."

The tall person who had confidently passed the test chimed in with a smile, "I think the computer was just too intimidated by my towering presence, so it passed me."

I couldn't help but join in, saying, "And as for me, well, I got a little 'help' with those tricky questions. Teamwork, right?"

As we exchanged glances, we couldn't help but burst into laughter, even shedding a few tears in the process. We were well aware of why he hadn't passed the test, but there seemed to be yet another layer to this enigma. So, we offered him comfort and assurance all the way, promising that next time, he would breeze through.

And, as the jokes went, he might as well have mistaken the gas pedal for a coffee maker! The car wasn't ready for his "expresso" driving style!

* * *

And there it was, the big day of the practical driving test. I had to rise at the crack of dawn, ready to conquer the challenge of steering the ancient and manual Mercedes. To be perfectly honest, I was more accustomed to this relic of a car than I was to a fresh cup of morning coffee.

My confidence was as high as the sun in the sky, and I wasn't losing sleep over whether I'd pass or fail. It was Saturday, a day of promise, and Kenneth, with a day off on his hands, came with me. We were set to embark on a post-test road trip to Elbasan, which was enough to put a twinkle in my eye and a grin on my face.

As I took the driver's seat, the adventure kicked off in high gear. I deftly shifted into first, mastering the clutch and gas pedals with the grace of a ballet dancer. The cast of characters in the car included my trusty instructor riding shotgun, and the evaluator, our "specialist" who held my fate in their hands, perched in the back seat.

Picture this: I was cruising along, acing the maneuvers with the poise of a seasoned pro, and then, just as we were about to tackle a turn, a colossal truck rumbled into our path. I decided to nudge a bit closer to the curb, perhaps a bit too dramatically, because my instructor's reaction was something to behold. Panic overtook him, and he lunged for the steering wheel, trying to save us from an imaginary disaster.

Well, it turned out that I had everything under control, even if my instructor didn't quite see it that way. From his perspective, it was a white-knuckle ride of epic proportions. But the reality was, that I had nailed the test, including the parking. In the end, I believed I had failed, but it seemed my instructor's nerves were the only thing that needed a bit of steering.

Sixteen

Chapter 16

It was another day, another reason to celebrate, as December's chilly days drew near. The sight of the festive New Year decorations brought joy. Yet, the most heartwarming moment was watching Liam carefully placing ornaments on the Christmas tree. His small hands and rosy cheeks radiated curiosity and love.

"Mom, where should I put this ball? And where should I place this star?" he asked.

It was so beautiful that it made me wonder, "Will I be here next year with all of you? Will I be healthy and a part of your lives again? Oh, how I wished for it. I longed to be there, with all of you. It didn't matter if we occasionally argued or bickered; as long as I could be there."

On New Year's Eve, we all gathered: my parents, my aunt, Flora, my brother, my brother-in-law, and Claudia, my other cousin. As we prepared to take a group photo, I playfully quipped, "Hold on, hold on,

I'm not ready. Let me fix my hair. Ha-ha."

Isn't it wonderful to be with loved ones during the holidays?

Everyone laughed, and we took a photo when we were finally ready. I used to dislike photos, but now I understand their significance in our lives. Perhaps we'll look at them one day and think, "I was there. We had a beautiful time. Life has its moments that are worth living for. Maybe I'll delete these photos in the future, maybe I won't. But those moments were beautiful."

* * *

After the New Year's celebration, it was my third therapy session. So, this time I had the opportunity to leave with Kenneth and be ready for the morning check-up. Every morning, I would get my check-up done so that my doctor could examine me before proceeding with the treatment. That morning, I entered my least favorite place in my entire life once again. Every time I stepped in there, my whole body would shiver. A terrible feeling of anxiety and stress would grip me, without understanding why. Dr. Nola greeted me with her usual smile.

"Rachel, I see that your values are a bit low, but it's normal due to the chemotherapy. Nevertheless, we can continue with the treatment as they are still acceptable. Please, I know it's hard, but you must try to eat well and remain very calm."

"Thank you, doctor, I will do my best," I replied with a smile.

Kenneth had to go to work, so I had Claudia staying beside me. I knew that having her by my side would make everything easier. She was such a free and cheerful spirit that I could say she was born in the wrong place and time. She had a fantastic voice and was very talented in music. She sang and played the flute and the piano. I don't know how many times she made me cry by playing the Titanic music on her flute. Her words were words of hope and support, even though she could be a bit scatterbrained at times. But we understood each other well because probably, we're both Gemini signs. Now, we fight like any cousins, even though we've grown up. She's a girl, somewhat tall like me, with long black hair and small, mesmerizing hazel eyes.

Of course, with her cherished company, time passed unnoticed. But this was the third therapy session. I couldn't say that my body was reacting with more energy; in fact, my energy was declining. I no longer had the strength I used to, but Claudia helped me move forward. Holding my hand and leaning on her, we managed to step into the darkness of the night that had enveloped the city. We hailed a nearby taxi. After entering the house, I said to Claudia in a soft and tired voice,

"Please give me a call when you reach home. You know I worry when we go out at night."

"Don't worry; I will let you know when I arrive. Are you sure you don't want me to come inside your house? Do you think you can stay alone until Kenneth comes back from work?" Her questions showed concern.

"Please, don't worry about me. I've gotten used to it now. I'm okay! Thank you for everything. Have a good night and call me when you get home." I replied in a weak voice.

"Okay, all right! I'll give you a call. Talk to you in a bit,' she said and left for her house in a taxi.

After a few minutes, Claudia called to let me know she had safely returned home. I changed into comfortable clothing and took a soothing sip of tea in an attempt to calm my restless mind. Fatigue weighed me down, and I couldn't wait for Kenneth to return from work before surrendering to slumber. Utter exhaustion enveloped me; all I longed for was to close my eyes and rest.

In the boundless, pitch-black abyss of the night, there was a pervasive chill in the air and a subtle taint of stagnation. I found myself enveloped by a disorienting obscurity. It was as if I were trapped within an impenetrable fog of smoke and shadows, struggling to discern anything in my surroundings. I squinted and strained my eyes, desperately seeking to pierce the enigma that surrounded me. This was a test of my patience, a battle against the oppressive weight of the unknown.

My breath grew shallower, and I felt adrift in that vast, desolate expanse. It was a desolation so profound that it left me with a haunting emptiness, an emptiness in which I grappled for meaning. I didn't feel pain or sadness; instead, I was in a state of numbness, an indescribable sensation. It was a feeling that compelled surrender, a release of everything, a relinquishing of all that was held tight.

I was utterly drained, my spirit fragmented and weary, as I lay there in the quiet of the night. That moment felt like an eternity. After walking for a very long time, I once again confronted the black shadow that had relentlessly followed me for so many years. Strangely, I felt no fear. I approached it slowly. I don't know why, but I knew I had to move towards it. It was as if it was gazing down at me from above. It was simply a dark figure, the tall shape of a man, yet still faceless.

Loomed above me, closely observing, contemplating what I would do.

This time, I wanted to surrender; I no longer wanted to try to escape. I was incredibly, incredibly tired. Tired with a forced smile, tired with unspoken words. Tired of my illness, which no one could discuss or share with me. In fact, I couldn't even admit what I had; I couldn't accept it. I was in a state of denial, and I wasn't even aware of it. But I was exhausted, seeing smiling faces around me that perhaps when I wasn't present, were weeping silently.

How did they feel? Why didn't they speak? This silence made me feel much worse. And that smile I wore every day was so painful that, it felt like a knife gently piercing my heart. The pain was so severe that it became hard to breathe.

The shadow above me had extended its hand without uttering a word. Countless thoughts raced through my mind. I wanted someone to be there, to cry with me, perhaps even scream at the world, asking, 'Why?!' But I also wanted to escape; I didn't want to feel that everyone was happy as if nothing had changed. I wanted someone to say to me, 'Cry with me, release your grief, scream.' But no, I couldn't, I couldn't. No one heard my dreadful, desperate screams."

I was so close, so incredibly close to accepting his unseen, black hand and telling him to stop everything around me. I didn't know how others felt about me; perhaps they felt worse than I did and were trying to appear strong for my sake. They might have been hiding in the bathroom or their rooms, weeping silently, but not with me. Who would cry with me in those moments when I felt so defeated? Who? Should I accept it or not, I felt his presence, and I wanted to put an end to it once and for all. Who would tell me to stop, that they understood and felt my pain? Who would tell me to simply let go of myself and the pain for a single second? Could I even do that? I couldn't do it with anyone. ..I was alone at home, alone in my most challenging moments…

Darkness enveloped everything. I didn't want to experience pain every time I smiled; no, I didn't want that…I grab that hand, and everything would cease to exist…

For a moment, I lowered my head into nothingness, and all the feelings of others, how they would feel if I were to give in at that moment, closed my eyes. Those feelings I had been trying to erase from the depths of my soul. They hurt me as much as taking a breath did. A pain of immense proportions had seized me. It was as if someone had grabbed me by the throat and said, 'Give up now, that's enough.'

I decided not to breathe for a while and focused on something else, my memories. My life hasn't always been dark. My life is precious. Even though it might not seem valuable to me at this moment, it is valuable to someone else. But there I was, shaken and torn, thinking that my life was valuable to someone else. Enough… Tears welled up, and then something urgent was trying to shake me…

The doorbell was blaring incessantly and urgently, barely allowing me to leave my bed.

A terrible and irritated shout came from Kenneth, 'Where were you until now? I had to leave work and rush here with a heavy heart. Your dad was crying on the other side, and you weren't answering the phone!'

His anger was so intense, unlike anything I had ever seen. Trying to soothe him with a soft voice and a faint smile, I mumbled, "'I'm sorry, I apologize. I had put my phone on silent, and that's why I didn't hear it at all.' 'That's why.'"

"People sleep until eleven in the morning, not until two in the afternoon. God! Get your dad on the phone; he's worried. I have to go to work, darn it!" He slammed the door behind him in frustration.

In fact, I remembered putting my phone on silent because I had been receiving calls very early, and this time, I wanted to sleep more; I was feeling very unwell. But now they were worried. I took the phone in hand and dialed my dad's number.

"Dad, I'm sorry I scared you, but I had the phone on silent, and that's why I didn't hear it ringing. I'm fine, don't worry; I just needed to rest." I rushed through all the words.

"Alright, alright, Ray, the important thing is for you to be well. You shouldn't sleep so late; it's not good for you. Now get out of bed and be ready to talk to your son on WhatsApp; he's eagerly waiting. Come on, get up!"

"Okay, I'm getting up, just let me brush my teeth first," I replied with a smile.

I went to the bathroom, still half-asleep. In fact, I was very tired because I hadn't been feeling well yesterday. I had taken three sedatives to avoid feeling my heart pounding so hard. I couldn't bear it. After finishing in the bathroom, I picked up Liam with the camera to greet him and see his face, which gave me the strength to not give up.

Seventeen

Chapter 17

The days and weeks passed by, each moment leading me closer to my final therapy session. I was filled with anticipation and happiness, but those four months felt like an eternity. I was determined to complete my therapy before celebrating Valentine's Day with Kenneth and his friends. I informed them that I wasn't certain if I could join their celebration, as I wasn't sure how my last therapy would affect me.

Like every morning, I had my tests done, and I diligently sent the results to my doctor. However, when she reviewed them, she delivered unexpected news. My values were not as good as they needed to be for the final session. The therapy had to be postponed. Despite the disappointment, she suggested I stay for the weekend, and after that, we could redo the tests to see if there would be any improvements.

Since the test results halted the progress of my final therapy, we decided to embark on a vacation to Pogradec, a place closely connected to Korçë, which I can visit time and time again without ever tiring of its charm.

Pogradec, in winter, held a special place in my heart. As is often the case when we set off on a pleasure trip, I meticulously packed all my necessary medications, along with some toiletries and elegant attire. At that time, I didn't have an epinephrine auto-injector, but I was always prepared for the unexpected.

In the morning, we woke up early and began our journey to Pogradec, a three-hour drive from Tirana. Along the way, we made a few brief stops for coffee and water, but our destination beckoned. After securing our hotel reservation, we retreated to our room to refresh and prepare for a delightful lunch.

That evening, we were three couples: Kenneth and me, two of his friends, one accompanied by his fiancée and the other by his girlfriend. The two friends were twin brothers, and even then, I still struggled to tell them apart.

Have you ever been on a trip that had unexpected turns? Usually, that is me. Always but always something bad has to happen.

We sat down for lunch at one of the charming lakeside restaurants. Given that it was only lunch, there was no need for us to put on our finest clothes. Instead, we opted for comfort and dressed casually.

Kenneth couldn't help but tease, "Rachel, I see you're wearing your 'eating pants' today."

I chuckled and replied, "You know me too well. Gotta make room for this delicious food somehow!"

Our friends joined in on the banter. Marta, one of Kenneth's friends, said, "Hey, I'm with Rachel on this one. These lakeside restaurants have the best food, and we're here to enjoy it, right?"

Leonard, the other friend, chimed in, "Absolutely! Comfort over style any day."

As we enjoyed our meals, the conversation flowed, and we shared funny stories and more jokes, making the lunch an even more enjoyable experience.

But I knew all these laughs, alcohol, and jokes would lead to something I didn't want. I felt it. Something bad would always happen to me, and I was always on guard and prepared.

Kenneth said with a grin "Come on, don't be such a worrywart. It's just a bit of fun."

I smiled "I hope you're right."

We went to the room to change and rest a bit before heading to dinner. Our room was quite comfortable, with a double bed and two nightstands. There was a mirror, a TV, a small hallway, a closet, and a luxurious bathroom. It had a relaxing shower that helped so much with the body aches.

Kenneth looked around "Not too shabby, huh?"

I nodded "Not at all. This room is great."

In the spacious bathroom, we also had a Jacuzzi with music and room for two. After filling it with warm water, Kenneth and I got in to relax. It was fantastic, and the soothing music and Jacuzzi definitely led to what you're probably thinking…Well, it depends on what are you thinking…

"This is what I call a perfect way to unwind," Kenneth winked

"I have to admit, it's quite nice," I chuckled

I dozed off for a few minutes. Well, yes, I dozed off. The journey was long, and I wasn't in a super fantastic condition, so sleep got the best of me.

Kenneth jokingly said, "Hey, don't fall asleep on me!"

"I'm here, don't worry," whispered a drowsy

Plus, we had a few drinks and two beers. So, one thing led to another.

Time was ticking away as we prepared for dinner. I chose a snug black dress with a side slit, but since I felt weary, heels were out of the question. Instead, I went with white sneakers and a short white jacket, a blend of casual and classic. In the bathroom, I started with my eyes, accentuating my few remaining eyelashes with mascara. I continued to my eyebrows, defining my lips with a deep black pencil. Completing the look, I wore a wig under my black hoodie, highlighting the wig's beauty. A spritz of my favorite Armani perfume, and I was set.

Kenneth, as usual, wore jeans and a dark green shirt. We were both ready. Anyone seeing us would assume all was well. It seemed perfectly normal - that's how Kenneth approached everything as if everything was fine. We set out to secure a table at some top-notch restaurants, but they were fully booked, an oversight on our part. Leonard then decided on a less fancy but excellent food restaurant. The girls had a more casual style than I did. I felt overdressed that night, but I did it to boost my confidence. To remind myself that everything was okay. To keep going and never stop.

We were having a great time; you could see Bernard and Leonard, nearly tipsy. They had consumed so much wine. I had sipped on a little wine, no more than two red glasses. They began to sing and dance.

Bernard with a big grin "This wine is fantastic! What do you think, Leonard?"

"Absolutely! I haven't had this much fun in ages," Leonardo laughed

Around the table, the restaurant's owner came over, occasionally adding logs to the small restaurant's fireplace. The fire warmed the atmosphere on this cold winter evening, with just a bit of snowfall, as Pogradec and Korca are known for during the winter.

Restaurant Owner: "Enjoying your evening, folks?"

"Absolutely! The ambiance here is lovely," I replied

I tried a bit of different kinds of wine, something I hadn't tried before, and some eggfish. After a few minutes, I began to feel a significant warmth, so I went to check myself in the bathroom. But what did I see? I was covered in red welts, and I realized that something had caused an allergic reaction.

Worried but trying to hide it, I said to "Leonard, something's wrong. I've broken out in hives!"

Leonard Concerned answered "Oh no, let me see. You look pretty bad. Should we call an ambulance?"

I took a few allergy pills, but as it turns out, they weren't doing the job. The situation was getting worse; my breathing was becoming difficult, my tongue felt swollen, and I texted Kenneth (who went to the pharmacy to grab stronger allergy pills), "Forget it; we're going to the emergency room, I don't think the allergy pills are working."

I felt embarrassed for ruining dinner and that everyone had come for fun, but as always, something would happen to me or around me.

I started in a low voice "Leonard, I don't think the pills are working; it would be better to go to the emergency room. I'm so sorry I ruined dinner."

"Don't be sorry; your health is more important. Let's go," he replied

Concerned, he jumped out of his chair, and then, we all headed to the emergency room. He was driving so fast that for a moment, I felt like I was in a Fast and Furious movie. I was silently berating myself, but why should others get hurt because of me?

"Leonard, please walk more slowly; we all need to arrive there safe and sound," tried to calm him down.

He didn't say a word. Without understanding, he confused the route, and then he found it again. He stopped spectacularly right in front of the hospital, and there we were, finally there.

The doctors, as soon as they saw us rushing in, realized it was something truly urgent. They quickly directed us to a room and, in a hurry, examined me thoroughly. They gave me adrenaline, prednisolone and I don't know what else. Then, a nurse arrived to put oxygen to help with my breathing.

He politely said, "Please move your hair a bit so I can place the oxygen."

"Sure, I'll move it now. Actually, I don't have hair, but I'll adjust the wig," I smiled.

Looking at me with a puzzled expression, he remained silent, simply placing the oxygen and saying, "You should feel better now."

"Thank you!" I replied.

Leonard was so drunk that he lay down on another bed in the room, muttering, "Doctor, doctor, I don't feel well either!" He was joking, but I asked him to calm down and lower his voice fearing of causing a problem.

After a few hours at the hospital with oxygen and adrenaline, we could finally return to the hotel, of course, after I was out of danger. Well, my precautions never let me down. Next time, never dare to try something you haven't eaten before. One thing is for sure, you never get bored with me...

We stayed another day in Pogradec, we enjoyed it. But of course, I didn't dare to try new foods, considering what had happened the previous night.

But I knew that after a day, I had to undergo tests again and send the results to the doctor, who would decide if and when I would have another therapy.

* * *

The next day, after I did the tests and sent them to the doctor, she asked surprised, "How is it possible that your levels have risen so quickly?"

Thinking that it might have been due to the prednisolone and adrenaline, I replied, "Maybe it's because of the medications they used on me in the emergency room after I had a severe allergic reaction. They administered adrenaline, prednisolone, and oxygen."

"Yes, that's the reason. Since prednisolone and adrenaline increase all the values. Um, okay. Then, in these circumstances, today, you can have your final therapy." the doctor confirmed.

"That's fantastic!" I responded, unable to contain my joy that it would be the last time I'd see this hospital or at least the chemotherapy part.

The doctor added, "After we finish this therapy, your hair will start to grow back in a month. And after a few months, you'll need to schedule the next MRI."

"Thank you so much for your help and support, Doctor. Thank you!" I couldn't believe that this would be my last time, at least until now, until those moments.

The future was uncertain, but for that day, it would be my last day fighting this disease. But I had to see how everything had gone and the results of the next MRI after a few months.

* * *

I knew that the results of this MRI would finally reveal whether there were still traces of the tumor or not. I was stressed, and as always, I couldn't sleep all night. I was terrified at the thought of starting everything over. After several months when I had the MRI again, which never created a pleasant feeling for me, except for stress and anxiety, it ended this time as well.

After we got the results, I had to consult with my surgeon, who was the first to participate in my complicated operation, Dr. Muhamet. Those moments of waiting while he was examining the MRI felt like a dreadful eternity. I was trying to read his facial expression.

"Everything is fine. Your body is clean. You are completely healthy, and the tumor is gone. Live as normal as possible and eat healthy. I wish you only the best," the doctor confirmed, and for the first time, I saw a smile on his face.

I thanked the doctor and left his office. I gave the good news to Kenneth, and he, as always, with no reaction, said, "I knew it would turn out well. You have nothing. You're okay."

* * *

Walking alone, I thought to myself, "Is this true, what I just heard? I am not sick anymore? Oh God, thank you, thank you for everything. I was happy that at least my health was good. After some time my hair had grown back a bit, and I had styled it in a rebellious and very interesting way. My small head looked so beautiful and natural with such short hair.

Oh, I almost forgot to tell you that, I changed my job. Even today, I ask myself why I did that! But I believe that everything happens for a reason. It wasn't a very pleasant experience, but I stayed to learn as much as I could. Do you remember the movie "The Devil Wears Prada?" Well, it was somewhat like this story. But this will be a story for another book to write… The most important thing now is that I am healthy, I am still alive, still taking a breath, still living.

I want to tell all of you who read this book, "Please pay attention to your health. Do things that make you happy. Avoid stress and live every moment in this challenging but worthwhile world. Do not give up! Stay positive! Fight every second!

Life is an endless challenge. Fight until you are alive! Take a breath, open your eyes, and keep fighting! Never give up!

Surrender is the fate of the loser. You are not a loser; you are a warrior, a survivor…"

About the Author

Ina Zeneli, born in Albania in June 1989, is a versatile author whose passion for storytelling began in childhood. Her books, including "The Boy Who Talked His Way into Trouble," "Tickles, Toys, and Tunes," and "Hanna The Job Quitter," cater to both children and adults, offering a wide range of stories.

In her debut novel, "Looking Death in the Eyes," Ina skillfully blends reality and imagination to create a captivating narrative that blurs the line between the ordinary and the magical, exploring the themes of curses and miracles.

Ina has poured her heart into this story, hoping that Rachel's journey will inspire readers and remind them that hope perseveres even in the toughest times. This book celebrates the strength of unity, the inspiration it brings, and the remarkable impact of unwavering support.

Ina sincerely thanks her readers for choosing to be a part of this adventure.

You can connect with me on:
- https://twitter.com/Ina54377403
- https://www.facebook.com/InaZeneli
- https://www.pinterest.com/inatace
- https://www.tiktok.com/@inazeneli_writer

Also by Ina Zeneli

9 798822 782523